BILLIONAIRE'S DOG NANNY

MISHA BELL

♠ MOZAIKA PUBLICATIONS ♠

CHAPTER 1
LILLY

How the hell is he hot? Everything about Bruce Roxford is ice cold, from his arctic blue eyes to the frosty frown on his lips. Even his dark, sleeked-back hair has a cool, blue-black sheen to it instead of the usual warm brown undertones.

"Yes?" he demands, pointedly not opening his front door any wider.

Why is he acting like his security people didn't announce who I was? Not to mention, we have an appointment—and it's not like there are random people coming and going from his massive estate.

Doing my best not to shiver from the chill he exudes, I say, "I'm Lilly Johnson."

No reply.

"The dog trainer."

Silence.

"I'm here for an interview with Bruce Roxford?"

What I don't say is that the interview is just a pretext to give the heartless bastard a tongue lashing. His bank took my childhood home, so when I saw his ad looking for someone in my field, I knew it was fate.

Maybe I should just cuss him out now?

No. He'd slam the door in my face and have his security escort me off the premises. I need to have him as a captive audience. Before seeing him in person, I figured I'd lock us in a room and read the note that I've carefully composed for the occasion. That way, I wouldn't forget any insults or accusations. However, now that I'm face to face with this huge, broad-shouldered male specimen, I'm less sure about being alone with him, especially in a hostile situation.

He folds his muscular arm in front of his face and frowns at his A. Lange & Sohne watch. "You're late. Goodbye."

The words hit me like shards of hail.

"Late by five minutes," I retort, proud of how steady my voice is. "There was traffic and—"

"Traffic is as predictable a fact of life as taxes." He starts to close the door in my face.

I suck in a big breath. No time to read my whole spiel. A quick version will have to suffice.

Before I can let loose any vitriol, a blur of black fluff darts out from the tiny sliver between the door and its frame.

A guinea pig?

No. It's wagging its tail and licking my shoes.

Oh, right. It's a puppy—which makes sense given the ad.

My heart leaps. This is a long-haired Chihuahua—and a gorgeous one at that, with a silky pitch-black coat, white fur on its chest, a face that reminds me of a tiny bear, and brown patches above its eyes that look like curious eyebrows. Better yet, the lack of yappiness and ankle biting thus far makes me think this might be the friendliest member of this particular breed.

I crouch and pet its heavenly fur. "Hi there. Who are you?"

The puppy flops over, revealing that he's a good *boy*, as opposed to girl.

A bittersweet ache squeezes my chest as I scratch the little bald patch on his belly. It's been five years since I lost Roach, the canine love of my life, and he too was a Chihuahua—just much bigger, less friendly to strangers, and with a smooth coat.

To this day, whenever I come across a new member of this breed, a touch of sadness tarnishes the joy of meeting a dog. Luckily, because they are small, few people formally train Chihuahuas, so I've never had to pass on a client because of this. In any case, the joy quickly wins out as I move my fingers to scratch the puppy's fluffy chest, and he starts to look like he's mainlining heroin.

"You like that, don't you, sweetheart?" I croon.

As usual, my imagination provides me with the dog's response—which, for some unknown reason, is

3

spoken in the impossibly deep voice of James Earl Jones, a.k.a. Darth Vader:

Do I like belly rubs? That's like asking if I like howling at the moon. Or licking my balls. Or eating a—

Somewhere far above me, I hear someone blow out an exasperated breath.

Oh, shit. I forgot where I am. It's a common occurrence when dogs are involved.

Straightening to my full height (which, admittedly, is barely five feet), I stare up challengingly into my nemesis's blue eyes—which look wider now, like fishing holes in an icy lake.

"How did you do that?" he demands.

I nervously tuck a strand of hair behind my ear. "Do what?"

He gestures at the tail-wagging Chihuahua. "Colossus is never friendly. With anyone."

So maybe he *is* typical for his breed. I grin, unable to help myself. "Colossus? What is he, like two pounds?"

"Two and a half," he says, expression still stern. "Do you have bacon in your pockets?"

Feeling like I'm on trial, I pull out my pockets to show they're empty. "I never feed dogs bacon. Even the safest kinds have too much fat and sodium, not to mention other flavorings that—"

"Okay," he interrupts imperiously.

I blink at him. "Okay what?"

"You've got the job."

CHAPTER 2
BRUCE

The tiny creature—and I'm not talking about the puppy—raises one of her impressively fluffy eyebrows. "I've got the job?"

"Yes."

She will be my first-ever tardy employee, but between Colossus liking her and the bacon diatribe, she's the best candidate I've seen thus far. As ridiculous as it is, this position has been harder to fill than that of my CTO.

"Just like that?" she asks as she gently picks up the puppy, who, to my shock, lets her do so without a single biting attempt.

It took an entire week before he allowed me to reach for him without chomping on my fingers—and none of my staff have yet achieved this feat.

I open the door wider to let her step inside. "One of my trade secrets is my ability to choose the right person for every job."

The other fluffy eyebrow joins the first. "Are you sure your trade secret isn't your modesty?"

I pretend not to have heard. I have no idea why Colossus likes her. He's clearly a horrible judge of character. I bet it was something stupid, like the fact that she's the tiniest human he's ever met, which makes him feel like a bigger dog. Or it could be as simple as the fact that she smells nice. As she passes by, I detect notes of cherries and incense in her perfume, along with something floral.

She waits until I close the front door before setting Colossus down on the floor—an attention to detail that I appreciate. We don't need the dumb puppy running out.

"What on Earth are those?" She points at the pee pads that span the whole house, like a blue carpet.

I grimace. "Colossus is not housebroken."

She wrinkles her dainty nose. "I prefer the term 'domesticized.'"

Though my eyebrows are vastly inferior to hers, I arch one anyway. "Is there a practical difference between a 'housebroken' and a 'domesticized' Chihuahua?"

She narrows her hazel eyes at me. "Is there one between 'abrasive' and 'jerk?'"

If that's an attempt to insult me, it's as weak as her attempted lesson in linguistics. "'Domesticize' makes it sound like we're taming a wolf."

As usual, my mind boggles at the idea of Colossus sharing 99.9% of his DNA with a fierce killing machine. Then again, the puny human in front of me and I share even more DNA, which just proves how much difference that tiny percentage can make.

Her nose wrinkle spreads to her forehead. "I don't like the word 'tame' either. I associate it with training methods that use coercion and abuse."

My teeth clench involuntarily. "Are there people who use such methods?"

Dumb puppy or not, if I caught anyone coercing or abusing Colossus, it would be the last thing they ever did.

She looks at me like I've asked her if the tooth fairy is real. "There are even people out there who organize dog fights."

Such people are lucky I'm only in charge of a banking empire and not the whole world. Otherwise, the fuckers would be dog food.

"Tell me about *your* methods," I demand.

"Positive reinforcement all the way." She kneels next to Colossus and scratches under his chin—which he seems to enjoy disproportionally, judging by the mad wagging of his tail. "I find something the dog likes and provide that something whenever I see a behavior I want repeated."

I get that. In essence, it's not all that different from year-end bonuses—which I excel at providing. Or praise—something people claim I'm bad at.

"I'll have to arm you with the oatmeal cookies that he goes crazy for," I say gruffly.

The puppy likes the ones my chef makes, but he loves my own recipe as if it were laced with opiates.

She rises to her feet. "Does he like peanut butter?"

"He'd sell his soul for it. Then again, he likes anything edible—and many inedible items as well. So far, I haven't come across anything he doesn't like."

She cocks her head in a way that reminds me of Colossus. "Even citrus?"

I snort. "He *adores* oranges. Begged for a lemon too, but I heard they can cause stomach upset, so I didn't give him any."

She glances at the puppy in disbelief. "What about vegetables?"

"Cucumber seems to be his favorite food."

She gives me a skeptical look. "What about greens?"

I feel illogically proud as I say, "I've given him arugula, spinach, and kale—and he's chomped it all down."

"With no stomach upset?"

"None."

"Wow," she says. "That's great. Food-motivated dogs make a trainer's life easier."

Before I can warn her about overfeeding Colossus, my housekeeper runs in, my ringing cellphone in her hands.

"I'm so sorry, Mr. Roxford," she says. "This thing keeps going off."

Judging by the ringtone, it's someone from the office, and they wouldn't dare bother me if it weren't something to do with the cryptocurrency we're developing—my passion project at the moment.

"I'm going to take that." I snatch the phone and look at my new employee. "In the meantime, you can decide when you're going to move in."

CHAPTER 3
LILLY

pick up my jaw from the floor as the lady from *Downton Abbey* skedaddles, and "Mr. Roxford's" long legs carry him away.

Move in? For puppy training? Is he insane, or has my hearing gone haywire?

I pull my phone out of my purse and reread the ad that got me here.

Oh, wow. Near the bottom, it says this is a live-in position. Since all I'd wanted was one interview, I hadn't bothered reading that far down.

I peer at Colossus. "Do you know why he wants a live-in?"

The tiny puppy sits on his butt and gives me his full attention—something I usually have to teach other dogs.

Does the sea of pee pads not give you a clue, or are you going to shame me by making me say it? Oh, and if I do say it, can I please, please, please have an oatmeal cookie? With peanut butter?

Right, of course. Puppies go potty at night. A lot. Also, the "many inedible items" was most likely a reference to the dog's ripping and consuming of the pee pads... or toilet paper... or gravel.

Yep. Puppies are like clumsy vacuum cleaners with teeth. And alarm clocks without a snooze button. Still, hiring someone to train a puppy around the clock is something only a billionaire would do.

An evil, greedy billionaire who's made his fortune stealing homes from ordinary people like my parents.

I grit my teeth and remind myself to be patient. I *will* tell him off. Any minute now. As soon as he returns. I should've told him off already instead of gabbing with him about my training methods, but the super-cute puppy threw me for a loop.

At least I think it was the puppy, and not the fact that the man I've hated for the past year has turned out to be way too good-looking in real life—if you're into the whole tall, dark, muscular, symmetrically featured, blue-eyed rich jerk with an icy vibe thing.

Which I'm totally not.

It's the puppy. It has to be.

Said puppy wags his adorably bushy tail. I crouch and give him another belly rub, whispering, "It's not your fault your daddy is a monster."

A monster who needs to be told off.

I get my note out and review the most salient points.

Yeah. Here we go. No more indecisiveness.

As soon as Roxford comes back, I'm going to hit him with my words.

Then again, maybe I should locate him right now, rip his phone from his hands, and let him have it. Alternatively, I could tape this note to the front door and skedaddle. Or even take the job and—

A clearing of a throat brings me back to Earth.

Damn him. Even his stupid throat is hot—all muscly, sinewy, and with a prominent Adam's apple that just begs you to give it a lick or a nibble.

"Here." He steps so close to me that a hint of lemongrass and lime pleasantly tickles my nostrils. "Since I was in my office, I printed the contract you are to sign. Assuming you find the rate acceptable."

I scan the stack of papers he's handed to me until my eyes land on said rate, at which point I nearly drop the document.

Given Roxford's propensity to throw people out of their homes, I assumed he'd be cheap, offering minimum wage at best. But I was wrong.

Veterinarians don't get paid this much. Neither do gynecologists, urologists, or proctologists. Nor high-end escorts… as far as I know.

It's the kind of money where I'd be an idiot not to at least consider forgetting why I actually came here— and most of my other scruples and principles as well.

No. What am I thinking? I can't possibly train the puppy of the man responsible for the loss of my childhood home. That would be like sleeping with Hitler. Or bathing Putin. Or clipping Mel Gibson's toenails.

But the money…

And there's no sleeping with or bathing the enemy involved…

Unless… wait a sec. Going back to escorts and proctologists, is it possible he's expecting something from me that isn't puppy training? Or at least not the kind of puppies I normally work with? I've heard there's such a thing as BDSM puppy play…

Holy crap. Is this why this is a live-in position with a contract?

Is this mansion where his Red Room of Pain is?

How insulting… and yet bizarrely tempting.

No, not tempting. Disgusting—that's what I meant.

Although, come to think of it, there's a real Chihuahua puppy in front of me, so—

"Well?" he demands, narrowing his icy eyes. "Does this work for you?"

"The pay seems reasonable," I manage to squeeze out. "But—so there's no misunderstanding—what services do you expect from me in return?"

He looks at Colossus. "I want him to earn the dog equivalent of a PhD in Rocket Science… from Harvard."

"You mean, turn him into a service dog?"

Why is a part of me disappointed about the lack of sketchy sexual favors?

Roxford gives me a look that implies I'm a total

idiot. "What kind of a service dog could a tiny creature like Colossus become?"

"Oh, you'd be surprised."

"Surprise me then."

"He could warn diabetics of low blood sugar, stave off anxiety attacks, and so on."

He eyes me dubiously. "And you can train him to do those things?"

I don't think this is the time to disclose that while training service dogs is my goal in life, I currently don't have much experience. Instead, I opt for my most impressive achievement. "Well, my cousin is a fertility consultant who owns a Yorkie not that much bigger than Colossus, and I taught her how to tell if a woman is ovulating."

For the first time, the corners of his eyes crinkle in a hint of a smile. "You taught the dog or your cousin?"

"The dog, but if I had enough lychee macaroons, I bet I could train my cousin as well—assuming she'd be okay with getting all up into her customers' crotches."

He full-on smiles, and it's glorious. If you could bottle that smile, I bet it could cure many sad things in the world, like depression, anxiety, and constipation. Too bad you can almost hear the creaking as his facial muscles bend in an unfamiliar-to-them way. I doubt he unleashes this smile more than twice per year.

"So…" He sheaths the glorious smile much too soon. "How about you start by teaching him the equivalent of grade school?"

"That would be learning to potty in proper places, plus things like 'sit,' 'stay,' 'wait,' and 'drop it.'"

He glances at the ocean of pee pads splayed out to the horizon. "Make the bathroom part your top priority."

If I were a dog, my hackles would be rising. "Do you always bark orders at people without so much as a 'please' and 'thank you?'"

He gives me an unapologetic stare. "If you want pleases and thank-yous, we'd have to communicate via email... and I'd have to halve your rate."

Wow. "No, *thank you*."

"Great. Then rid me of the pee pads in the house by the end of the week."

"End of the week?" I snort. "That would be tricky even if I moved in *today*."

He doesn't miss a beat. "Then you are moving in today."

I gape at him. "What? No! I have other clients. I have my own place, so I'd need movers. I—"

He waves his hand dismissively. "I'll have my assistant find your clients someone else. I'll also have him hire movers for you in an hour."

Shit. He's serious.

There's no way I can move in today... can I? I haven't even decided to take this job. In fact, I know I shouldn't take this job. Even if he weren't the man who deprived my parents of their home, I'd need at least a week to evaluate all the pros and cons. The latter are countless—and the asshole boss is just the tip of the iceberg. There's the overly cute Chihuahua that I might develop feelings for if we spend any more time together—which is bound to lead to a heartbreak similar to what I experienced when I lost Roach. There's the—

"If you move in today, I'll give you a sign-on bonus," the aforementioned asshole says. "Your daily rate times one hundred."

My jaw hinges open.

"And if you get rid of the pads by the end of the week, you'll get another bonus—your daily rate times a thousand."

Holy puppy pee. I know he's bullying me with the money, but I can't say no to these kinds of numbers. Service dog trainer school and certifications aren't cheap. Neither is my parents' rent, which I'm helping them with.

In fact, he's offering the kind of money that would let me help them with a down payment on a new house.

My heartbeat picks up pace as excitement sizzles through my veins.

It would be the ultimate poetic justice if I used his money to help the very people he evicted.

But no. I can't possibly make this decision so impulsively. I have to think it through. I have to decide if this makes sense. I am not a "seize the moment" kind of person. I like to think before I act, to analyze all the potential implications and—

His face darkens with impatience, his arctic eyes

turning colder as he stares at me, and I blurt in panic, "If I say yes, where am I going to stay?"

His gaze is pure ice now. "If?"

"Yes. If." I raise my chin, ignoring the sweat trickling down my spine. "I'm not staying in a cupboard under the stairs, à la Harry Potter."

"You will stay in the biggest guestroom." He gestures into the distance, where, possibly miles away, is my room-to-be. "Any other demands?"

Now that I'm closer to making a decision, I feel a modicum calmer. "I refuse to call you Mr. Roxford."

His face is hard to read, so I have no idea if he's kidding when he asks, "How about 'sir?'"

I scoff. "Hell, no. And before you ask, forget things like 'master,' 'mister,' 'my lord,' 'big cheese,' 'monsieur,' 'señor,' 'pan—'"

Did he just growl?

"Call me Bruce." The name is said through his teeth. "I presume you want me to call you *Lilly*?"

I swallow hard. I like how he says my name—even if he is trying to make fun of it.

"That's correct… *Bruce*." Ugh. Why does *his* name on my lips feel so forbidden and intimate? I reach for my snark with effort. "And when you do say my name, try not to sound like you're eating a lemon."

He bares his teeth. "Let me show you to your room."

He leads me deeper into the mansion. The pee pads crunch under our feet, and I hear the pitter-patter of Colossus following us.

We pass a library bigger than the one in *Beauty and*

the Beast. The room after that is filled with an armor collection that wouldn't look out of place in a museum. We keep walking, and I keep gawking, especially when we pass what appears to be a small movie theater.

He stops walking suddenly, so I bump into him, and Colossus bumps his little wet nose into my heel.

"Here." Bruce opens a set of tall doors.

Tail wagging, Colossus rushes inside the room and disappears under the California king-sized bed.

I stare. The luxurious guestroom is double the size of my whole apartment, with furnishings reminiscent of a fancy hotel and the high ceilings of a cathedral.

Bruce steps in and opens another door. "This bathroom will be yours."

The bathroom is five times the size of the one I have back home.

"This will work," I say in an understatement of the century. My own accommodations for guests are a pull-out couch and a freebie toothbrush I got from the dentist.

He closes the bathroom door. "I'll have the movers clear the room and bring your things."

Clear the room for my things? "No need, thanks." That would be like swapping a sleek Lamborghini for a horse and buggy made by the inventors of the Nissan Cube.

He looks around as if seeing the furniture for the first time. "You want to use the room as is?"

I nod vigorously. "So long as the sheets are clean."

There's liquid nitrogen in his gaze. "The sheets are new. So are the towels. Ditto for the toothbrush and—"

Colossus emerges from under the bed, a moth the size of his face in his mouth.

"No!" Bruce shouts. "Don't eat—"

Too late. The little Chihuahua crunches on the moth, then swallows it.

Considering their relative sizes, this would be like me catching and swallowing a pigeon.

"Bad dog," Bruce says sternly.

Colossus plops on his butt and looks at his human with big, soulful eyes that show zero guilt.

What's wrong with fluffy sky raisins? They eat clothes, I eat them—this is what my voice-twin Mufasa meant by The Circle of Life. I'd be willing to trade the next one for an oatmeal cookie. Especially a flying cookie.

Instinctively, I place myself between Bruce and Colossus. I imagine a man who could steal my childhood home is capable of kicking a puppy. "Moths are considered safe for dogs to eat."

"Oh?" Bruce imbues the syllable with so much sarcasm I want to smack him.

"Moths don't carry any known diseases and are nontoxic." I know this because Roach *loved* to eat moths, and flies, and—ironically—roaches too, when he could catch them.

Bruce crosses his arms. "He must listen when I forbid him to eat something."

"How not tyrannical," I say caustically.

His nostrils flare. "You don't think a creature with a

brain the size of a walnut could use help when it comes to making such decisions?"

"Size of a walnut?" I examine Bruce's head with an exaggerated thoroughness. "That would make your skull even thicker than I thought."

Bruce bares his teeth—which happen to be perfect, damn him. "Is that right?"

"You betcha." I glare up at him, forgetting all caution. "And if you wanted to eat shit, I'd let you."

"You know what, *Lilly*? Forget the job. You're fired."

"Great." I dive into my purse to pull out the note. If I don't get the money, I'm at least going to give him an earful.

This might even be for the better, in fact. Inhaling a deep breath, I rattle out, "You are a heartless machine— and the embodiment of what's wrong with the world. How could—"

Colossus whines pitifully, stopping me in my tracks.

I kneel fast. "What's wrong?"

Could that moth be hurting him? He didn't chew it much, so it's feasible he could get stomach upset from that.

The puppy looks from me to Bruce, then whines again.

Oh, shit. I know this behavior. He—

"He doesn't like the arguing," Bruce mutters under his breath—which is what I was about to conclude.

I feel terrible. Of course, the puppy will pick up on

the hostility in the room. Dogs are social beings, after all. I was behaving like a Bruce.

"Everything is okay," I croon to Colossus. "Bruce and I were just speaking with passion."

The puppy calms down impressively quickly. When I would accidently get Roach into these types of situations, he'd mope for a couple of minutes.

Even though Roach is long gone, I feel a pang of guilt about the fights I had with my ex in front of him. I don't feel as bad about today's situation because the blame rests on Bruce.

Speaking of, I get up and narrow my eyes at him. "Any chance you could *not* be your awful self around the puppy after I leave?"

"You're not leaving," he says through his teeth. "The dog likes you, and I have no idea why."

"Wait, what?" I gape at him. "Are you saying...?"

"Forget what I said. You still have the job. For now." He looks as if the words cost him more than this mansion.

My heart leaps—and not just because of the money. In no time at all, what I've feared has come true: I'm already so attached to this Chihuahua that leaving him alone with his cold-hearted owner isn't something I'd feel right doing.

"That is, if you can behave yourself," he adds before I can breathe out a sigh of relief.

It takes everything I have to stay calm for Colossus's sake. "Behave myself?"

"You will be cordial from now on. Or you *are* out of here."

Deep breaths. I can do this. "On one condition." My voice is a touch sharper than I intend. "Same goes for you."

He gives me an incredulous stare. "I wasn't the prickly one."

"No?" I take another deep breath and let it out. "See? I let that go." Even though I could've told him that if he opened the Wikipedia page under "prick," he'd see his own picture.

"It's a start," he says. "Now, will you deign to answer my earlier question?"

Stay calm. "Which one?"

He glances at his fluffy ward. "Can the dog be taught to not eat something I don't want him to?"

"Yes. That's what I was talking about earlier when I mentioned the 'drop it' command. Just bear in mind, it's much easier to make a dog drop inedible objects."

"Understood." He gestures around the room. "Why don't you examine everything and put together a list of what you need brought here?"

More like, he's finding it too hard to stay cordial with me past that one question.

And that's fine.

I feel the same way.

I'm already looking around when Bruce leaves and Colossus dutifully follows.

Wait. The puppy went with him? Either it's Stockholm syndrome, or he really isn't so bright.

CHAPTER 4
BRUCE

When I need to calm down, I like to read, box, or cook.

Reading is out because I don't think I can concentrate on a book right now. Boxing seems wrong in this particular context: I'm angry at a tiny creature, and a female at that, so if I found myself picturing her face on the punching bag, I'd have to hand over my man card.

That leaves cooking, and I know just the thing I will make—the oatmeal cookies that Colossus and I love.

I've got to hand it to the dog. When food is involved, his IQ suddenly rivals the combined scores of Lassie, Scooby Doo, and Cujo. As soon as I pull out the first ingredient, rolled oats, he gets super excited, and I'm sure he's sleuthed out what's about to happen.

Ignoring him for now, I take out flaxseed, zucchini, almond butter, and maple syrup—ingredients cleared by the vet.

The dog whines.

"Fine." I hand him a little taste of each of the ingredients, and he devours them like they're the first foods he's ever tasted.

"Now wait," I say sternly and proceed with my work.

By the time I've made the batter, I already feel calmer. I'm not even sure why I got so riled up in the first place. My best guess is because it's been a while since I've dealt with someone as disagreeably unprofessional as Lilly. I'm her client, yet she speaks to me as though she hates my guts—but we only met today.

At least, I think so.

No, I know so.

She's not the kind of woman I'd forget. Not with those fluffy eyebrows arched above those greenish hazel eyes, and that feistiness.

For some unfathomable reason, my lips curve into a smile, and my cock gets hard.

I look down. What the fuck, cock? What's with this reaction? Do you think Lilly and I are a couple? Are you hoping that makeup sex is on the horizon?

I can't think of a more ridiculous notion than the two of us dating. I mean, Lilly's attractive, in a gamine sort of way, but who cares, given how contrary she is? Also, not that it matters, but I don't plan on dating anyone while the cryptocurrency project requires all of my time and energy. Either way, once I do get around to dating, it won't be someone like her. Prickliness aside, she's my employee, and therefore out of the question. She's also a decade younger than I am and is at an age when all she probably wants to do is take selfies at nightclubs, post said selfies on her social media, and obsess about the likes of Justin Bieber or whoever the girls are squealing about these days. And she's way too dainty. I'd feel like a fucking ogre if we did anything... which we won't.

Fuck. That image doesn't help with the fucking erection.

Maybe opening a 375-degree oven will help?

Nope. Unbelievable.

I stick the cookies in and set my phone timer to ten minutes.

The puppy sits patiently, hypnotizing the oven.

I step around him and lock myself in the adjacent bathroom.

Motherfucker. My cock is still hard, despite everything. You'd think *I* was the hormone-driven twenty-three-year-old instead of Lilly.

I try thinking about government banking regulations. Nothing. I switch my focus to IRS audits. Still hard. I bring out the big guns—people loudly chewing and slurping their food.

Unbelievable. Even that doesn't help.

Gritting my teeth, I fist my cock—the one surefire way to get rid of this nuisance.

As I go on, I do my best to finish in ten minutes while keeping images of Lilly from my mind's eye.

The time limit is a success.

The image suppression is a huge failure.

CHAPTER 5
LILLY

After scanning the room, I put my list of belongings together—and it's not a long one. Pretty much just my clothes and shoes. And my video games, of course.

Just as I'm about to leave, a thin man with a Mario-like mustache walks into the room.

"Hello, Lilly." The way he says my first name makes it clear he usually addresses people in a more formal manner. "I'm Mister... I mean, Johnny. Mr. Roxford's assistant."

"Whose assistant?" I refuse to call that asshole "Mister" anything.

Johnny twirls his mustache. "You're kidding, right?"

Taking pity on the minion, I say, "You must mean Bruce."

"Yes. Mr. Roxford." This time, he pulls on the mustache nervously, and it's a wonder no hairs get plucked out.

I scoff. "Yes. Bruce."

"Right." He reaches for the mustache again but stops halfway. "He asked me to get your list of things to move."

I hand him the sheet of paper in my hand.

Not pulling away his hand, Johnny says, "And your keys, please."

I snatch the list away. "Don't I get to supervise the movers?"

Johnny's left eye twitches. "Mister... *Bruce* said if they break anything, he'll replace it. He also said it's imperative that you start Colossus's training immediately."

"Well," I hiss. "Looks like for the first time in his life, Bruce isn't going to get his way."

And if he wants to fire me for this, so be it.

———

As Johnny, his mustache, and I walk through the mansion, I detect a delicious aroma that makes my stomach growl.

When did I last eat?

We enter the kitchen, and I spot the source of the yummy smell—a tray of cookies Bruce is taking out of the oven.

He cooks?

Nah.

Some personal chef must've left those in there, and

he's just taking them out. Serious domestic effort for a billionaire, either way.

Then my pulse jumps.

Colossus is near the table with a cookie in his mouth.

"Is that hot out of the oven?" I shout, leaping toward the puppy. "He'll get hurt!"

Bruce steps in my way. "That's the first batch." There's a twitch in his jaw. "I obviously waited for it to cool before giving it to the dog. What kind of a negligent sadist do you think I am?"

The worst kind—but I don't say this because we agreed to be civil only minutes ago.

"FYI, she insists on overseeing the move," Johnny tattletales.

Should I tell him snitches get stitches before their mustaches get shaved off?

"I'll allow it," Bruce says magnanimously.

"You'll allow it?" I grit out, forgetting about cordialness for a hot second. In a calmer tone, I say, "If it pleases Your Highness, I'll be back before you can say 'the top one percent.'"

Bruce turns his broad back to me. "Just get your possessions so you can start on your duties. And it's the top point-zero-zero-one percent."

———

All the way back to my car, I brainstorm some clever comebacks to Bruce's last comment, but the best I can come up with is: *I hope Colossus "dooties" on your foot.*

My car looks comically small in the giant driveway in front of the mansion, and as I start my route back home, I actually pay attention to the details of the massive estate.

There are two lakes on opposite sides of the mansion—creating gorgeous views from all angles. On the far side of the nearest lake is an untouched forest with a deer herd frolicking around. It's a marvel Bruce hasn't hunted them to extinction, as his kind are so fond of doing. Near the second lake, there is a garden maze and a golf course. Walking the dog around here must feel like strolling through a luxury resort.

My phone rings.

I check who it is.

Ah. It's Aphrodite, my cousin. And no, we're not Greek, so my aunt can officially be considered a child abuser for naming her daughter that.

"Hey, cuz," she says as soon as I pick up.

"Hey, Aphro," I reply with a smile. "Thanks for checking on me... a bit too late."

I told her what I would be doing, just in case Bruce went *American Psycho* on my ass.

She sounds worried as she asks, "Do I need to bail you out of jail?"

"I didn't actually do what I set out to do." I'm glad this isn't a video call, so she can't see me blush in shame.

"Why? What happened?" she demands.

I sigh. "He made me an offer I couldn't refuse."

She gasps. "He put a gun to your head?"

"What? No!"

"Well, that's what that phrase means in *The Godfather*."

I blow out a breath. "I'm pretty sure you can also use it in a situation where someone offers you a shit-ton of money."

"Hold on," she squeals. "Are you saying you're going to be working for the guy?"

I grip the steering wheel tighter. "As a dog trainer."

There's shocked silence on the other line.

"He's got a super cute puppy," I say defensively. "And the money is insane."

"What's your banker's name again?" Aphrodite asks in that peculiar way I dislike.

Knowing I will regret it, I tell her anyway. She types in a few keys, then whistles. "Super cute... *puppy*, was it?"

I bet she's looking at the picture on Bruce's Wikipedia page—which doesn't actually do the in-person Bruce justice.

"I know what you're thinking," I say. "And you're wrong."

"I'm thinking that if you wanted to snag yourself a billionaire, it was smart to meet with him on the day you're ovulating. Men are more attracted to us during that time window."

"Excuse me?" I force myself to slow down. I'm

approaching the estate's security gate, and the last thing I want is a reprimand from Bruce for putting one of his guards in the hospital. "What are you talking about?"

"You're ovulating," Aphrodite says, relishing the word. "When we saw you this morning, Uranus sniffed it out."

Grr. I shouldn't have given Uranus a chance to use his very particular set of skills on me. "Next time you need a dog trainer, I won't be there to help you," I growl, though I wonder if this stupid ovulation could explain why I find icy Bruce hot—in a purely physical sense.

"Don't be mad," Aphrodite says as I drive through the gate and turn onto the road. "I figured you'd want to know in case you happen to hook up with him. That way, you can decide what you want: to protect yourself from an unwanted pregnancy or the opposite."

"The opposite?"

"You know, trap a billionaire with a baby," she says helpfully.

I grit my teeth. "There will be no sex with that monster. And certainly no babies."

She sighs. "You need a boyfriend, and this guy is a billionaire who is easy on the eyes."

"I don't need a boyfriend, but if I did, the owner of the evilest bank in the world is the last man I would consider. Your aunt and uncle lost their house because of him."

"I'm sure he didn't personally handle their loan," she

says. "The argument can be made that they lost their house because they didn't pay their mortgage."

"I'm not going to argue this with you again," I say. "The owner of a business is ultimately responsible for what his company does. Anyway, even if he didn't own that cursed bank, I'd never date a client. And a jerk at that."

She hums. "I find it very interesting how much you've thought about this already."

I press on the gas a little too enthusiastically. "Have not."

"Protest too much?"

"No." I tap the brake. It's not worth getting a speeding ticket over this.

"Well," she says. "I'm sure you also realize that he won't be your client forever, and it's possible you don't know him well enough to be sure of his jerkiness yet."

Ugh. "Forget it, Aphro. Even if he magically turned into a nice person who owned a bunch of charities, his family would never let him date someone like me. They're the old-money kind of rich, while you and I are white trash."

"We're business owners," Aphrodite says defensively.

"Of tiny businesses," I say. "And our parents can't even say that much."

My dad does pool maintenance, and my mom cleans other people's houses; both work for a company owned by someone else. Aphrodite's mom is a hairdresser, and her dad was an anonymous sperm donor that her mom had a one-night stand with. Bruce's parents, on the other hand, are famous for philanthropy and organizing fundraisers in New York. I doubt I'd know what to say to them if I met them.

She sighs. "Our parents are lower, lower, lower middle class."

"Yeah," I say sarcastically. "Same income bracket as Joe Dirt."

"You know," she says. "Mood swings and irritability are very common during ovulation."

I groan. "Can you leave my reproductive organs out of the conversation, please?" Next time I'm over at her place, I'm going to train Uranus to pee in her shoes.

"Okay," she says. "But only if you tell me everything."

So I do just that, and it takes most of my drive home because when I get to the part where I'm moving in with Bruce, I have to reiterate my refusal to be Bruce's baby mama.

"I expect daily reports," she says when I'm finally finished.

"Sure." I hang up and park next to my dingy condo complex.

The movers are already waiting outside my door, and they look very high end, for movers. I didn't even know that was a thing. They call me "ma'am" and handle my crap with care—which makes me wonder if Bruce is paying them more than the stuff they're about to move is worth.

Either way, when it comes to my sex toys and video

games, I don't want the movers involved. When they're not looking, I sneak The Squirrel—a lipstick-sized clitoral vibrator—from my nightstand into a Converse shoebox where I keep such things, and then I disconnect my Nintendo Switch dock from the TV and put that and the console into a special carry case along with all of my favorite games.

"Can I help you carry that?" asks one of the movers, reaching for the shoebox.

I take a step back. "No, thanks."

"What about that?" He gestures at the game carry case.

"No." I step back again… and trip over my coffee table—which is when many things happen at once.

I flail my arms.

The shoebox and the carry case fly out of my hands.

A mover catches me before I break my back.

Another mover catches the bag with the games, but the side of the shoebox hits the coffee table and pops open, sending sex toys flying in different directions, with a few hitting the movers.

Oh, shit.

Someone kill me *now*.

Face burning, I extricate myself from my savior, snatch The Squirrel from the floor, and shove it into my pocket.

Except I miss the pocket and the thing falls on the floor again—causing me to have to bend over one more time.

Maybe it would've been better if I'd hit my head on something.

To my horror, the dudes pick up the toys nearest them, then nonchalantly stash them back in the shoebox.

Wow. Not a snicker, nor a wink, nor a chuckle. These must be the most professional movers in the world.

"Thanks," I mumble when the cursed box is handed back to me. "See you at the mansion."

I start escaping when I hear the one who caught me say, "If we don't see you, we'll just leave the stuff in your new room, and you can rearrange it after."

If I had any money, I'd give them a huge tip as hush money. The guy has to know I'm going to eat a meal and otherwise stall on my way back so that there's no way I'll face him and his crew ever again.

———

When I drive up to the mansion, the front door is closed and there's no sign of the moving truck.

Whew.

I ring the doorbell, and like a case of déjà vu, Bruce opens it, eyes even icier.

"What now?" I ask, reminding myself to stay polite.

He looks like he wants to behead me or worse. "Once again, you're late."

CHAPTER 6
BRUCE

illy clutches her possessions protectively. "How can I be late when I didn't tell you when I'd be back?"

The fact that she has a point only infuriates me further—but I rein it in since the dog is currently behind me. "Your new charge has had two accidents."

Her eyes turn slitty. "You mean *your* puppy?"

"You should've been here with the movers." Who left an hour ago.

"Am I not allowed to eat?"

She's been here for all of two seconds, but a thudding pain is beginning to form in my temples. "Next time you're hungry, speak to Chef Foxposse, or Mr. Cash, or Mrs. Campbell."

She mutters something under her breath resembling, "Of course you have a chef." Louder, she says, "I have no idea who any of those people are."

"You were in the kitchen with Mr. Cash," I remind her.

She smiles for the first time in our acquaintance, and I realize that it's possible to find teeth pretty. "His name is Johnny Cash?"

"Your unprofessionalism is showing." As a small peace offering, I reach out to help her with the shoebox she has in her hands.

She jumps back as if I were going to bite her nose off. "Don't touch my things."

I press my fingers to my temples, willing the pulsing ache to subside along with the anger I promised not to show. "You met Mrs. Campbell too," I say with forced evenness. "Assuming you can remember as far back as when she brought me my phone earlier."

Her teeth show again, just a hint of them, but it sure beats the hostility. "Is her first name Soup?"

My muscles tense and the urge to lash out is unbearable, but I have to remind myself that Lilly is simply making a stupid joke. She doesn't know about my issues with soup, or more specifically, with the act of other people eating it. Slurping it. Blowing on it. Sucking it up through their teeth—

Something of my inner struggle must show because she says, "Sheesh. I was just joking. Lighten up."

"You will treat Mrs. Campbell—and the rest of my staff—with utmost respect," I say. "Is that understood?"

She nods, but I catch a stealthy eyeroll. I pretend not to see it.

"Can I get through to my room now?" She lifts her things.

I move out of her way and gesture for her to enter.

When she steps into the foyer, Colossus greats her with such enthusiasm you'd think she'd been away for five years.

"I know," she says, stroking behind his ears. "I missed you too."

She sounds like she means it too—and that pleases me, though I'm not sure why.

When the greetings are done, I lead her to her room in silence—since that is the easiest way for us not to upset the stupid dog.

"Be in the kitchen in ten minutes," I say after I open the guestroom door for her.

"Wow. I get a whole nine minutes to settle into a new place. How generous."

"Fine," I grit out. "Make it twenty minutes. You can find the kitchen, right?"

She nods.

I'm a little skeptical, but if I voice that, a fight is bound to ensue.

I turn to leave, but Colossus doesn't follow.

Traitor.

Fuck. What am I thinking? It's a good thing the dog wants to spend time with his trainer.

Not to mention, if anyone can show her where the kitchen is, it's him.

CHAPTER 7
LILLY

put down the box and the bag.

Damn.

Seeing my possessions sprawled out around the luxurious room really hits home the mind-boggling fact that I've moved into my nemesis's mansion.

If someone had told me this yesterday, I wouldn't have believed it. I would've claimed that I'm incorruptible—that no matter how much money he'd throw at me, I'd stick to my guns.

Turns out, all it takes to wear me down is enough money to purchase a purebred dog on a daily basis.

Whatever. I'm here, so I might as well make myself comfortable.

The problem with that is that it took me years of careful consideration to decide the optimal place for each my things back at my small shithole. There's no way in hell I can replicate such a feat here in the measly twenty minutes I've been allowed.

Before I can panic, I remind myself that my priority are the things I'll need on a daily basis—like my clothes. I can find a good spot for the video games at my leisure—assuming Bruce allows me any.

I scan the room. There's a dresser *and* a closet, but at home, I only had the latter.

Where should my clothes go?

I pull out my laptop and start a pros and cons spreadsheet for the dresser option.

In the pros row, I put the fact that all of my stuff is foldable. In the same row, I add that a dresser is a luxury I didn't have back home, so it might be nice to utilize one.

On the cons side: my stuff could get creases.

Jumping back to the pros: a dresser is closer to the bed, so it would be faster to take things out in the morning.

Wait, there's a con I mustn't forget: the closet will let things keep their shape.

Hmm. There was that moth that time in my old room, but I'm not sure if they're more likely to eat things in the dresser or in the closet.

My phone beeps.

Great.

It's the timer I set in order to make sure I'm not late —which means I haven't unpacked a single thing in the allotted time.

Fine, I'll admit it. Sometimes, I find it hard to make a decision. But hey, at least it would be hard for a shyster car salesman to take advantage of me—not unless they were willing to field my million questions and wait a year for me to choose the hypothetical vehicle.

Opening the door, I take a step into the hallway—which is when a furry, tiny creature whooshes out from between my legs.

Wait a second.

I totally forgot that Colossus was in the room with me. I wonder what he was—

Oh, shit. What is that pink thing he's got in his maw?

Please, no.

But the truth is inescapable. He's got The Squirrel.

"Wait!" I shout.

Without turning or stopping, he wags his tail, which makes his opinion clear:

I've always wanted to chew a squirrel, but I'm happy to play this human-chase-puppy game instead.

The worst part is he's headed for the kitchen.

No. Embarrassing myself in front of the movers was bad enough, but if Bruce sees that sex toy, I'll simply—

I hear voices coming from the kitchen, one female and three male.

Oh, fuck.

Has Bruce gathered his staff to introduce me to them?

"Please, Colossus," I shout. "Stop!"

He wags his tail harder and speeds up.

I'll consider trading this toy for an oatmeal cookie. With peanut butter.

Right. A treat. I pat all my pockets, but I have nothing even remotely edible.

Grr. If I were already working with Colossus, I would probably be able to bluff him by holding my hand out like I've got a treat, but it won't work yet.

What kind of a shitty dog trainer am I? I gave the dog a chance at my boxes—and I don't even have a treat in my pockets.

The kitchen is looming ever closer.

As I sprint, I pray to Anubis, the Egyptian god with a canine head. *Please stop that puppy. I'll do anything. I'll always carry a treat from now on and watch the puppy carefully... and even foreswear masturbation. At least with toys.*

Nope. Colossus doesn't stop his mad dash.

Panting, I stumble into the kitchen, where the whole team is waiting for me, as I feared.

Should I pray to Anubis again, this time for the floor to swallow me?

A guy in a chef's hat with orangish hair and a similar shade of spray-tanned skin has a spatula in his hand, so he must be Chef Foxposse. Spotting the running puppy, he backs away as if he were afraid of dogs... or sex toys.

Johnny Cash and Mrs. Campbell are here as well, and they're gaping at Colossus's maw—so I can't hope they haven't noticed.

My cheeks burn so hot you'd think I've shaved them

with a pizza cutter and used pepper spray as aftershave.

The only one who leaps into action is Bruce. He grabs a cookie from the tray, crouches, and sternly says, "Drop that."

Chef Foxposse drops his spatula just as Colossus releases The Squirrel.

The toy rolls on the floor. If anyone hadn't already gotten a good look at it, they have now.

Oh, and it's vibrating. Because of course.

"Here." Bruce breaks off a piece of the cookie and rewards the puppy with it.

Colossus attacks the treat with an excitement that other dogs reserve for bacon, peanut butter, and cats.

This is my chance.

I leap forward to grab the toy, but Bruce snatches it before I get there and stashes it in his pocket.

Halting in my tracks, I catch my breath. I figure I'll need the power of speech to tell him off after he fires me.

Bruce looks at his watch. "Now that everyone is finally here, let me start the introductions." He gestures at me. "This is Ms. Johnson, Colossus's trainer."

"Please," I manage to squeeze out. "Call me Lilly."

Ignoring me, Bruce says, "Ms. Johnson, meet Chef Foxposse, Mr. Cash, and Mrs. Campbell."

Each of the aforementioned individuals bows when their name is called.

Bruce glances at his watch again. "I have a meeting. Get acquainted while I'm gone."

He turns on his heel and strides out of the room. Colossus glances longingly at the table where the cookies are, but when they don't magically fly into his mouth, he races after Bruce.

As soon as Bruce is out of earshot, everyone seems to exhale a relieved breath—which is as you'd expect when in the house of a dictator.

I clear my throat. "Nice to meet you all." *Please don't ask about The Squirrel. Pretty please.*

"Hi, Lilly," Chef Foxposse says with a smile. "You can call me Bob."

Huh. Chef Foxposse definitely sounds posher than Bob.

"You know me already," Johnny says and twirls his mustache.

He and Bob look at Mrs. Campbell.

She sighs. "If Mr. Roxford isn't around, you can call me Prudence."

"Good point," Bob says. "I'd also like to keep things formal when the boss is around." He grins at Mrs. Campbell. "That's just prudent."

The housekeeper rolls her eyes, then turns to me. "He's a much better cook than he is a comedian."

"Speaking of," Bob says. "For dinner, would you mind having ricotta gnocchi with white truffle?"

Is he kidding? "That sounds wonderful." Like a dish in a fancy restaurant.

"How about grape panna cotta for dessert?"

"Even better."

Damn it. Even though I ate on the way here, my mouth is watering.

Looking pleased, Bob asks, "In general, which foods are your favorite?"

Johnny and Prudence exchange looks. I guess the chef asks this of everyone.

"I don't have favorites."

"Well, what kinds of foods do you like?" he asks.

I shrug. "I don't know."

Bob looks confused. "How could you *not* know?"

"Never decided," I admit. Not for lack of trying. "Whatever foods I try, I like."

"I'm asking so that I can make something to your taste," Bob explains. "So we'll have to narrow that down."

I shrug. Unless he's a psychic, this is a tricky undertaking when it comes to me.

"What's your favorite breakfast?" he asks. "That should be easy, right?"

I sigh. "I could never pick."

He takes off his hat and scratches the top of his balding head. "Do you at least have a preference between savory and sweet?"

"I like both." That's the best answer I can provide without whipping out a spreadsheet.

He pulls a paper out of his pocket and glances at it. "How about Eggs Benedict?"

"I love it." My mouth waters even more.

Bob glances at the paper again. "How about buttermilk waffles?"

"That sounds wonderful." If he keeps this up, I'll start drooling like a bulldog.

Bob grins. "There you go. Two days' worth of breakfast is now settled. The eggs will be served with homemade smoked salmon and my take on hollandaise sauce. The waffles will be served with caramelized apples, apple cider glaze, vanilla whipped cream, and cinnamon streusel topping."

When is dinner again? This is what it must be like for the food-motivated dogs that I train.

Johnny curls the left side of his mustache. "Those are the breakfasts you're making for Mr. Roxford, right?"

Bob shrugs. "She's undecided, so why not make my life easy?"

"I don't mind," I say. "What else is he having?"

Bob hands me the whole menu, and everything on it sounds amazing, so I agree to it wholesale and hand the paper back.

Bob pockets the menu. "Thanks. If only Prudence and Johnny were so easy."

Johnny releases his mustache indignantly. "Most of the things on that list would give me heartburn from hell."

"And I'm watching my figure," Prudence says. "Unlike Mr. Roxford, I don't sweat for an hour in a boxing ring every day."

He's into boxing? Thanks, Prudence. Now instead of fantasizing about all those meals, I'm salivating at the image of sweaty Bruce.

I clear my suddenly thirsty throat. "So what's the food situation? Is it served at a specific time?"

"You can eat anytime if you're willing to use the microwave." He wrinkles his nose. "But if you want your meals fresh, which I highly advise, you should get on Mr. Roxford's schedule."

Prudence looks around furtively. "Just make sure not to eat in front of him."

Johnny pales and nods at this so profusely his mustache flaps like butterfly wings.

"Why not?" I ask.

The three of them exchange odd glances, but not a single one explains.

Not that it's hard to figure this one out. We're the help and should eat downstairs with our own kind, like they do on *Downton Abbey*. The fact that this is Florida and there is no downstairs is irrelevant.

"Before the boss comes back, can we talk about Colossus's food?" Bob says pleadingly.

"You cook his food?" I ask worriedly. Dogs have different nutritional needs than humans, and I doubt they teach that at culinary school.

Bob nods. "I do. Had to consult a veterinary nutritionist and everything."

Whew. "So... what did you want to talk about?"

He pulls out a paper and hands it to me. "Do you think he'll like these?"

I goggle at it. The paper is another menu, and the dishes on it are as fancy as what he's making for Bruce. The good news is the ingredients listed sound safe for dogs. "I think Colossus is going to be thrilled about this."

"I hope you're right," Bob says. "I wish I could see his reaction as he eats."

My hand flies to my chest. "You haven't seen him eat?"

"That dog doesn't like anyone but Mr. Roxford," Bob says defensively. "If I'm around when he eats, he growls at me."

That's resource guarding, a common problem for dogs and something I'll have to teach the little guy not to do.

Prudence looks at Bob reassuringly. "When I take the puppy's bowls for a wash, they're always sparkling clean. I doubt he'd lick the plates so much if he didn't enjoy the food."

"Maybe not," Bob says, but he doesn't sound too sure.

"Give me time," I say. "After a little bit of training, I'm sure he will let you watch him eat."

Bob takes a step back. "Only if Mr. Roxford allows it."

Tyrant strikes again.

"Since we're talking about food for the dog," I say. "What can I use as treats?"

Bob pulls out a big box filled with goodies, including some of the oatmeal cookies.

"Just email me a tally of the treats," Bob says and hands me his card. "Mr. Roxford wants me to subtract the snack calories from the meals."

That's taking controlling to a new level, but in this case, it will be beneficial to Colossus's health.

"Let me call myself from your phone," Prudence says. "I don't have a business card."

After I give her my phone, Johnny's mustache puffs up proudly. "I *do* have a card." He hands it to me. "And if you need to email Mr. Roxford, send your missives to me."

Bob looks around furtively, then conspiratorially whispers, "Johnny's job is to strategically pepper words like 'please' and 'thank you' into Mr. Roxford's emails."

Johnny tugs angrily at his mustache. "I do a lot more than that. Who do you think organizes—"

"Gentlemen." Prudence hands me back my phone and nods pointedly in the direction Bruce went.

Faces panicked, the two men hush, and just in time.

Colossus runs back into the kitchen, tail wagging when he spots me, and Bruce follows, his chilly expression a huge contrast to the dog's happiness.

"I trust the introductions are now completed?" The question is really a command to shut the fuck up.

We nod—I reluctantly, the others obediently.

Bruce grunts approvingly, then states, "Everyone except Lilly is dismissed."

Bob, Johnny, and Prudence scatter like cockroaches.

Wow. Too bad Johnny isn't able to make Bruce's speech more polite, like he does with his emails.

Once we're alone, Bruce's expression turns impossibly colder.

Great. I get special treatment.

A litter of butterfly-sized puppies collectively wags their tails in my belly as I ask, "Should we talk about Colossus's curriculum?"

Instead of answering, Bruce crosses the distance between us. Then his hand dives into his pocket, and I half expect him to pull out a gun and shoot me.

At this close range, I wouldn't stand a chance.

When I see what he actually pulls out, it's worse than a weapon.

It's my vibrator.

Fuck.

With all those introductions, I managed to forget about it, but now a new wave of embarrassment turns my cheeks the shade of a baboon's butt.

Bruce shakes The Squirrel accusingly. "Colossus could have choked and died."

CHAPTER 8
BRUCE

Lilly looks down bashfully at the dog, and her blushing face makes me think of spanked butt cheeks—for some unknown reason.

Damn it. The last thing I want is to turn into a spanking-obsessed billionaire cliché.

"You're right," she says. "Setting down the box with the toys was an oversight."

She has a whole box of this stuff? I've never been this simultaneously infuriated and turned on, not even when I saw a naked woman in the crowd of Occupy Wall Street protestors years ago.

Taking a calming breath, I thrust the toy into Lilly's tiny hand. "Make sure this *never* happens again."

I would forbid her from masturbating completely, but I don't need the HR rulebook to know that is not something that is under my control... unfortunately.

"I'm sorry," she mutters, her face turning even more gorgeously red.

Was that an apology? From her? I'd better sell all my orange juice futures because it's going to snow here in Florida.

Lilly takes a decisive step back. She must've realized we were standing so close to each other that she was at risk of inhaling polluted-by-me air.

With a loud gulp, she shoves the toy into her pocket.

Finally. Seeing her hold it was much too interesting for my cock—which is all the more inappropriate given that the thing put Colossus's life at risk.

"I have treats now." She shakes a box in a clear attempt to discharge the tension in the air. "If I need to get something out of his mouth—something that will not be my fault next time—this will help."

Colossus looks up at her with that expression he's mastered: a mixture of starved and worshipful. I have no doubt he can smell the oat cookies inside the box and wants them. Badly.

Resisting the urge to snatch the box from her hands, I force calmness into my voice as I say, "Do *not* overfeed him."

She hides the box behind her back. "Bob already explained your thoughts on this—which are sound. I'll keep track of the treats and coordinate with him to adjust the little one's calories."

I'm annoyed that "Bob" talked to her about something that was on my agenda.

Wait, am I jealous?

No. This is a lot like when Bob looks glum whenever I tell him I've cooked something. No one likes their job encroached on.

"So." I sit on the nearest barstool. "You started to talk about your plans for the training. What are they?"

She climbs onto a stool near me. Once she's seated, her legs dangle well above the floor. "I imagine potty training is your top priority?" She gestures at the pads that surround us.

"Correct." Poor Mrs. Campbell could use a break from having to change those things every couple of hours. "How does that work?"

She glances at her small student. "Puppies go after meals, playtime, and naps. They also have certain tells before they need to go. I'm going to learn Colossus's tells so that I can take him outside as soon it's needed. I'll use treats after he does his business, which should help him learn that going outside is best."

Sounds annoyingly reasonable. "Will this stop him from having accidents inside?"

"It will help," she says. "But we also want him to feel like this whole mansion is his den because dogs have an instinct not to go to the bathroom in their den."

Huh. "How do we do that?"

She looks around. "We can restrict his access to all but a tiny part of the house, then slowly open it up. Maybe use baby gates, or a crate, or—"

"No." I rejected another trainer because he insisted on this "crate training" business, which sounds too much like dog jail for my tastes. "Colossus will have access to the whole house from the start. End of story."

I like to pace the mansion, and the stupid dog whines if he can't reach me.

She sighs. "Will you micromanage the whole training process?"

I shrug. "Only if you have stupid training ideas."

Her signature eyebrows meet in the middle of her forehead. "I guess we could create a bunch of safe spaces for him throughout the house. Put a doggie bed in every room, with some toys. He might get the den idea that way."

"Good," I say. "Come up with more solutions like that."

"Sure," she grits out, looking like she might grab the nearby steak knife and reenact a scene from *Scream*... on my privates.

Speaking of danger. "Follow me," I say to Lilly and risk turning my back to her despite the knife.

She and Colossus follow me all the way to the garage.

"This is where I keep everything related to walking the dog," I explain as Lilly scans my car collection with boggled eyes.

"Oh?" She checks out the storage unit I've dedicated for the task. "What's that?" She points at the special talon-proof vest I had made for Colossus—one with Mohawk-like spikes.

"That's for his safety. Eagles, hawks, and owls have been spotted on the estate."

"Ah." She examines the vest, looking surprisingly approving.

I guess now is as good a time as any to show her the other gizmo I had created earlier today. It's for her: a shiny child's bike helmet with a Mohawk that matches the one on the dog's vest.

"This should further deter the birds." I hand her the helmet.

She gapes at it. "Is it for me?"

"Yes. It should keep both of you safer." And if a certain someone looks ridiculous wearing it, that's just a bonus.

She keeps staring at the helmet without taking it.

With a sigh, I walk up to her, gently place the helmet on her tiny head, then strap it under her dainty chin.

Fuck. She smells like cherries and incense again, and I finally identify the flowery scent—roses.

She stares up at me, her lips parted. Lips that are like sirens singing their devilish songs. My breath speeds up, and heat moves through my body as some magnetic force draws me down toward her.

My lips are mere inches from hers when I realize she's holding her breath like she's afraid I might choke her, and her eyes are wide and filled with something suspiciously like panic.

Shit.

What am I doing?

I straighten abruptly and pointedly examine how she looks in the cursed helmet—as though that's what I was doing all along.

Unfortunately, despite looking like an extra from *Mad Max*, she's still unfathomably sexy.

She blinks up at me and touches her lips, as if on autopilot. Then she takes out her phone and uses the front camera to look herself over.

An annoyed huff escapes that tempting mouth of hers. "Anything else?" she deadpans. "Maybe I should be tarred and feathered before every walk, so the birds think I'm one of their own?"

"Actually, yes." I pick up an air horn and thrust it into her hands. "Use this if you see so much as a shadow. It should scare the birds, and I've instructed security to come to your rescue if they hear it."

I'll come too, with a shotgun, but she doesn't need to know that.

She shakes her head in exasperation, causing the spikes on her bird-deterrent helmet to jingle. "What else?"

"Don't go near the lakes," I say. "They have gators."

She scoffs. "Unlike you, I'm a native Floridian."

There. Much easier not to think about kissing that mouth when it spouts things like that. "How do you know I'm not a native?"

She winces. "If I told you I read up on you, would it boost your mastiff-sized ego?"

"No." Yet the idea that she was interested in learning about me *is* appealing.

"All I know is you worked on Wall Street for most of your career," she says. "Since that's in New York, I figured you're not a Florida man."

"That may be for the best," I say. "'Florida man' conjures up an image of someone getting a DUI on a lawnmower… and then trying to sell the officer meth during the arrest."

She narrows her eyes. "Just like 'New Yorker' conjures up an image of a rude, miserable, loud, snobby workaholic."

I scoff. "Rude? That's just what outsiders call the efficient way New Yorkers speak. Miserable? Never heard that one. Loud? It's a noisy city. Snobby? That's just what people without taste say about people who have it. As to 'workaholic'—that's precisely what a lazy person would label someone who's hardworking, driven, and ambitious."

The latter I know from personal experience. Just because I work eighty hours a week doesn't make it right for anyone to compare me to an addict. Hell, if the people around me were more competent, I would gladly not work so much.

"Right," Lilly says snidely. "I forgot 'argumentative.'"

She's got the stones to call *me* argumentative? "Seems like some Floridians are like proverbial pots. Us New York kettles have a term for that: 'putz.'"

"Isn't that term usually applied to males?" she snaps.

I shrug. "Yes, but when the tiny shoe fits, exceptions can be made."

Did she just stomp said tiny shoe?

"Anyway," she says, and I can see she's making an effort to stay civil. "If you're done with the insults, I think Colossus and I will go for that walk now."

"Great idea." I open the garage door. "And remember, stay away from those lakes."

She rushes off, leash in tow and without so much as a thank you.

I wasn't teasing her with the gators bit. We've got some that are so big they wouldn't just eat the dog— they'd have her too, for dessert.

An unwelcome image of *me* eating her sneaks into my brain—and I don't mean cannibalistically.

Fuck.

Just like that, I'm hard again.

CHAPTER 9
LILLY

When the garage door closes, I gape at the puppy at my feet. "Did I dream that, or did Bruce and I almost kiss?"

Colossus cocks his head.

Kiss? Is that kind of like butt-sniffing? Either way, I'm not an expert. Now—on a completely unrelated note—can I call you two Mom and Dad?

No way was that an almost kiss. He probably wanted to bite my head off—literally. Even when I'm at my most attractive, I'm no billionaire bait, and with the hideous helmet he's making me wear, no sane male would want to come anywhere near me.

I scan the gorgeous landscaping, the pathways, the gardens, and the lakes in the distance.

All empty.

Good. No one is around to witness my shame.

Someone clears his throat from behind a sphere-shaped bush.

So much for no one seeing me in the dorky headgear.

The guy who steps out is about my father's age and has the most weather-beaten skin I've ever seen outside of pirate movies. "Hello," he says. "I'm Mr. Hornigold, the landscape architect."

Is that a fancy term for "gardener?"

"I'm Lilly," I say. "The canine instructor."

Colossus growls at the newcomer. Crap. I'll have to socialize him quickly, or else this will only get worse.

"I know who you are," he says. "Mr. Roxford wanted me to tell you that if the puppy does a number two, you don't need to pick it up. One of my people will do it."

"Got it," I say with a forced smile.

Seriously, though? How rich do you have to be to have "people" who clean up after your dog for you?

The growling intensifies.

Not good.

"Hey," I say to the gardener. "Do you mind helping me with the dog's training for a minute?"

Looking reluctant, he nods.

"Here." I toss him a piece of the cookie. "Please hand it to the dog on an open palm."

Kneeling, he does as I say, but he looks so scared you'd think he were dealing with a rabid pit bull.

Colossus stops growling and approaches the cookie.

"Yes," I croon. "Being friendly pays off."

The puppy eats the cookie and sniffs the guy's hand for a second.

"Can I go now?" the gardener asks.

"Yes. Thank you."

As the man departs, Colossus looks at me with a confused expression:

I thought he was evil incarnate, but that cannot be. Oatmeal cookies are like crucifixes—they ward away evil.

Grinning at him, I tug lightly on the leash and say, "Let's go."

With a tiny huff, Colossus pitter-patters over to the nearest patch of grass, plops down on his stomach, and begins ripping apart a dry leaf.

"That's cat behavior," I tell him sternly. "Doggies walk."

He ignores me.

"Let's go." I tug on the leash again.

Nope. He clearly hasn't been trained to walk on a leash.

I sigh. It sucks that I have to escalate the situation so soon, but I can't help it. I take out another piece of the cookie and show it to him.

Just like with the gardener, the change in the dog's demeanor is instant. Leaping to his feet, he locks eyes with me like a crazed hypnotist and wags his tail.

"Good eye contact," I say. "Usually, I have to train puppies to do that."

He wags his tail harder.

Does that mean I get the cookie? Please, pretty please? Pretty pretty pretty please?

Still holding the treat, I take a step forward, then another, dangling the morsel as bait.

The dog takes a few steps too, eyes never leaving the object of his desire.

"Good boy," I say and give him a tiny crumb.

Getting the picture, he walks some more, eyes still not on the road.

About a block later, nature finally calls, and Colossus runs up to a palm tree and hikes up his little leg comically high.

"Good boy," I gush. "Such a good boy." I give him a bigger piece of the cookie to get my point across.

He makes satisfied growly sounds as he devours his reward, then walks over to a patch of grass and does a more serious bit of business.

"Yes. Good job," I exclaim enthusiastically and give him more cookie.

Again, he attacks the treat ravenously, like he's been starving for a week.

Hmm. He just might be the most food-motivated dog I've ever met, which will make him easier to train.

Despite what the gardener said, the urge to clean up after the dog is strong, but I resist.

"Now we can go home," I tell Colossus, then lure him back to the garage with a few more chunks of cookie.

Removing our punky gear, I take him back into the house. He immediately zooms away, and I have to run to catch up.

"Dude!" I shout. "Where was this energy on the walk?"

He doesn't stop.

I chase him all the way to the library, where he runs up to Bruce, who is sitting in a comfy recliner and reading a book.

Damn it. How is it that the book makes him look even sexier? This is particularly odd since I'm more of a gamer than a reader.

Spotting the dog, my icy employer full-on smiles again—and it's as magnificent as before.

I clear my throat.

The smile vanishes so fast I start to doubt it was there in the first place, and he puts the book away before I can glimpse the title.

"I only get to read for a few precious minutes per day," he growls. "Is it too much to ask not to be disturbed?"

"Colossus ran here after our walk," I say defensively. "Did you want me to just let him roam the house unsupervised?"

"How was the walk?" he demands, ignoring my question.

"Informative," I say. "Among other things, I'll have to teach Colossus how to walk like a proper dog."

Bruce rubs his temple. "I thought he just didn't like walking with me."

"You've walked him?" I ask.

Bruce rises to his full massive height and folds his arms across his powerful chest. "Why is that so surprising?"

"Because you've got people for everything. Why not this?"

"I've walked him on a regular basis." With the angry way he grits out the words, it's a marvel Colossus doesn't whine again. "Like I said, I thought it was something about the way I was holding the leash."

I purse my lips. "How were you holding the leash?"

Bruce rolls his eyes. "How am I supposed to show you that?"

Hmm. "I think you could benefit from a lesson I give all my clients."

They all find the lesson somewhat odd, but he doesn't need to know that.

He narrows his eyes. "A lesson in dog walking?"

"Exactly. A walk is a collaboration between the dog and the human. If both know what to do, it works best."

He checks his watch. "Can you cram this lesson into twenty minutes?"

I nod. "We'll need the leash and some space—ideally carpeted."

"Follow me," he commands and returns to the garage for the leash. Afterward, he takes me to one of the few closed doors in the house.

"You're not coming in," he says sternly to Colossus before opening the door.

The puppy cocks his head and shows no sign he understands.

"The command is 'stay,'" I say. "And he doesn't know it yet."

With a sigh, Bruce crouches and with a straight face says to Colossus, "The rug in this room is a seventeenth-century antique and costs millions."

What? I don't think *I* want to step on such a thing, let alone allow a puppy to do so.

"I have an idea." I take a cookie piece and crumble it in my hand. "This will keep him busy." I toss crumbs all around the corridor, and Colossus goes berserk trying to collect them.

"Nice trick." Bruce opens the door and allows me to enter first.

I hesitate. The carpet looks to be Persian, with a pattern of circles and leaves.

"Can I step on it?" I ask, hovering my foot over the edge.

"Without shoes," Bruce orders and takes off his own loafers to demonstrate—in case I'm that slow.

Shit.

Am I wearing that sock with a hole in it?

I slide my sneakers off to check.

Yep.

Only one solution here—I take the socks off too.

Bruce stares at my bare feet in confusion. "Is that for the lesson?"

"Sure," I lie and step on the carpet.

Wow. It feels so warm and comfy under my feet you'd think it were made of clouds.

Maybe this is where the legends of flying carpets came from?

"What now?" Bruce demands.

I take a breath. "Now I'll pretend to be the dog—and you'll walk me."

CHAPTER 10
BRUCE

D id I just hear that correctly? She will pretend to be a dog?

Maybe this is a really odd, self-deprecating, jokey way of calling herself a bitch?

No. She means it literally. Why else would she be turning the front end of the leash into a loop and lassoing it around her midsection?

Fuck me. Said rope wraps under her perky little breasts, pushing them up for my already-overactive cock to admire.

"Here." She hands me the leash handle.

Stunned, I take what is offered, still unable to believe my eyes.

Little do I know this is only the beginning.

She kneels in front of me, like she's about to make some of my recent fantasies come true. Then she gets on all fours—which is the start of even more fantasies.

What. The. Fuck?

Is this a seduction attempt? Her perfectly shaped ass is on display, which seems to corroborate this... but what's with the leash? Does *she* think I'm that kinky billionaire cliché?

"Now," she says over her shoulder. "Show me your leash technique."

So maybe this isn't BDSM. Otherwise, what she's doing would be considered topping from the bottom. Still, whatever this kink is, I might just be into it. My cock is almost painfully hard.

She takes a four-legged step. Then another. Her ass shakes so temptingly I want to growl—or rip those jeans into shreds.

After she takes the next step, the leash goes taut.

"You're supposed to walk with me," she says. "That or press the button to give the leash some give."

I gape down at her. "What the hell is going on?"

"I'm the dog, you're the walker," she says in a snarky tone that calms my libido a little—one or two percent, tops.

"I got that," I bite out. "Why would you structure the lesson this way?"

The idea that she's done this with other clients— male clients—makes me furious... which is just as illogical as the sudden urge to order her to do this with me and no one else going forward.

She turns and looks up, just as she would if we were going at it doggy-style. "My training philosophy is inspired by the Golden Rule: only do onto dogs what I'm okay experiencing for myself."

"That makes a warped kind of sense," I admit grudgingly.

In fact, I've been following something like her philosophy all this time, which is why, for example, the dog eats food made by my chef.

"And you said you couldn't describe how you use the leash," she continues. "So now you can show me."

"Fine," I grit out.

"Finally," she says with an eyeroll. "Now let's see you walk me, and then I'll do you."

She wants me to be on all fours? That's another kink altogether, and one I'm decidedly not into.

One problem at a time. I readjust my erection so that I'm able to trudge behind her slowly. "Ready."

She crawls. I follow, keeping the leash loose.

"Great job," she says. "Now let's pretend you don't want me to go there." She gestures at the edge of the carpet. "There might be a squirrel, or something I shouldn't eat."

I pull on the leash as I would with Colossus in said scenario.

"No," she says sternly. "That's too hard. You could choke him."

I grit my teeth. "Maybe if he wore a collar, yes, but he wears a harness. At most, I'd lift him."

"You should learn the technique that can apply to all dogs. What if someone asks you to walk their bigger dog?"

She has a point. The same way I got saddled with

this dog, I could end up with another one down the line.

Apparently, I can't say no to some people.

"Go for the squirrel again," I order.

She does, and I could swear she shakes her butt as she crawls—a move that sends shockwaves through my throbbing cock.

With an iron effort of will, I pull the leash gently.

"That's better," she says. "But really, what you're going for is a little tug."

I do my best to tug.

"Almost there," she says.

Rolling my eyes, I pretend that a feather has landed on my hand—resulting in the tiniest micromovement.

"Yes," she says excitedly. "Just like that."

Of course. First, she gets on all fours, and then she sounds like she's getting fucked. If anyone from my staff were to come into the room at this moment, they'd be convinced I'm harassing her, even though the truth is closer to the opposite.

"Show me what you'd do if I were to lie on the grass." Matching actions to words, she lies down—in a pretty good imitation of how Colossus drives me mad on walks.

"Come," I say gruffly and do a micro tug. "Let's go."

She gets back on all fours and starts moving, so I keep the leash loose.

"Wrong," she says sternly.

"What are you talking about?" And does she not

realize she's in a perfect position to get her butt spanked?

"When he does what you want, you have to give positive reinforcement."

"Good girl," I growl through my teeth.

She stops and gives me a seething glare over her shoulder. "You realize dogs don't speak much, if any, English, right? They go by tone, and yours is saying, 'I'm going to murder you.'"

I fill my lungs with air, exhale to relax, and then pretend I'm speaking with an infant as I say, "Good girl."

"Better," she says. "Though, given him hiking his leg when he pees and all that, I'd wager Colossus identifies as a boy... but then again, it's hard to be sure."

"I obviously wasn't being woke," I snap. "I was giving *you* the reinforcement."

"In that case, don't call me 'girl.'" She pushes up to her feet. "Your turn."

CHAPTER 11
LILLY

"No," Bruce barks—which hey, is in the spirit of him playing a dog.

"Putting yourself in the dog's shoes is the best way to learn," I explain.

His lips press into a white slash. "I'll just rely on my imagination."

I rub my eyebrows because I feel a headache coming on, only to recall that I shouldn't draw attention there. People like Frida Kahlo are famous for their prominent eyebrows, but I consider mine man-deterrents.

Not that I care what this particular man thinks.

Nope. The opposite. In fact, maybe I should fluff them up in front of him?

"What, no comeback?" he asks.

I snort humorlessly. "Do people like you even have an imagination?"

"Do people like you have any tact?" He stomps off the carpet and slides his feet into his shoes.

"I'm tactful enough not to call you a fucking asshole," I mutter as I put my own shoes on.

"You have ten more minutes," he says. "Let's walk and talk."

I sigh. "What about?"

Without answering, Bruce opens the door. Sure enough, Colossus is waiting in the hallway, his tail wagging a mile a minute.

I shut the door behind us before the puppy can ruin the million-dollar rug, then grin down at him. "Which of us did you miss?"

As if in answer, the little traitor playfully taps Bruce's loafer with his paw, then arches his butt.

"That pose means he wants to play," I explain. "And yes, it *was* the inspiration for the yoga pose."

Bruce digs in his suit jacket pocket and pulls out a plush monkey the size of a mouse. "Fetch." He tosses the toy.

Colossus chases after the toy but doesn't bring it back.

"I can teach him that," I say.

Bruce sighs. "That's another thing I thought dogs just did naturally."

"Some figure it out on their own," I say. "I'm just going to speed up the process."

"Right," he says. "And that's what I want to talk to you about. What other lessons are on your agenda?"

"I'm thinking 'sit,'" I say. "With 'drop it' after that."

"What else?" He picks up the toy that Colossus abandoned and hands it to me.

As I take the thing from him, our fingers brush—and it feels like a lightning strike has spread throughout my whole body, leaving all my muscles tingly and my senses out of whack.

What the hell? Did we pick up too much static electricity on that insanely expensive carpet?

Stuttering, I walk and talk, enumerating all the things that I can teach dogs in general and the pros and cons of familiarizing Colossus with each skill.

"Are you always this indecisive?" Bruce interrupts when I'm halfway through explaining the benefits of teaching Colossus the 'down' command.

"Why would you ask that?" I mean, it's true, but he's picked up on it based on almost no evidence and that's beyond annoying.

"Because an expert typically just tells you a course of action. By giving me all the pros and cons, it sounds like you want *me* to decide—which would be like me asking you what my bank should invest in."

I almost add, "Or whose house to steal," but stop myself in time. Instead, I say, "Fine. I will decide."

It will take a lot of angst and effort, but I can do it.

Hopefully.

"Why not just teach him everything you know?" Bruce demands as we step into a room that seems to be dedicated exclusively to video conference calls—with a giant screen on the wall and a fancy camera pointing at a comfy chair in the middle.

I shrug. "If a big dog leans on a person, it's a problem. If a Chihuahua does the same thing, it's considered cute."

Bruce opens the nearby laptop. "Teach him what's considered good behavior for all dogs, no matter the size."

I feel a surge of relief. Teaching everything means I don't have to cherry pick, thus avoiding all those decisions.

Bruce descends into the chair as if it were a throne and then bends down to pick up Colossus, who seems to know the drill because he gladly hops into Bruce's outstretched hands.

Seeing the little creature held in those large hands tugs on something in my chest—which is ridiculous.

"You can take an hour break," Bruce tells me imperiously.

Hey, that's more polite than "you're dismissed."

I'm turning to leave when a video call shows up on the screen that I'm now facing—and Bruce must accept it because a person appears on the screen.

It's a gorgeous woman with shampoo-commercial dark hair, mascara-commercial blue eyes, and a Botox-commercial smooth forehead.

Hmm. Maybe this isn't a call after all. Maybe this is a movie, and she's the newest starlet?

"Brucey, sweetie," she chirps. "Who is that?" She points at me.

So... this is a call after all. And now I get it. She and Bruce must be a unit—which makes sense since outside of Hollywood and runways, you most often find women like this as billionaires' trophies.

"This is Lilly," Bruce says. Turning to me, he adds, "This is Angela. She's invested in Colossus's life, so she might have questions for you at some point."

An illogical jealousy burns my chest. It must be that I'm beginning to feel possessive over Colossus, and it bugs me that she has more right to claim to be the little guy's mom than I do.

Shit. They're both looking at me expectantly.

"Pleasure to meet you, Angela," I squeeze out through clenched teeth.

"Likewise," she says. "I'm glad Peanut finally has a nanny."

Colossus's ears perk up. He probably thinks he heard "peanut butter."

Who the hell is Peanut? Since she's just mentioned a nanny, I would have to guess it's a child. Their child? I don't like the sound of that… purely because kids make dog training harder, of course.

But hold on. If they have a kid, where is he or she? Also, I truly hope Peanut is just a nickname, like Brucey.

"How many times do I have to tell you?" Bruce growls at Angela. "He now goes by Colossus."

Wait.

Peanut is Colossus… but that would mean—

"I'm not a dog nanny," I say indignantly. "That's not even a thing. I'm a canine training specialist."

Angela examines me with narrowed eyes. "What's the difference?"

I narrow my eyes back. "You hire me if you want to train a dog to be a nanny for your child. And I guess if a dog nanny were a thing, you'd hire her if you were too busy to be a good parent for your dog."

Angela's stare turns icy—something she must've learned from Bruce. "Sometimes you get a dog, but life happens."

I open my mouth for a violent rebuttal, but Bruce states, "Lilly was just leaving."

Ah. Right. Dismissed. Lifting my chin, I stomp out of the room.

If those two do reproduce, it will be the spawn of Satan.

CHAPTER 12
BRUCE

As soon as Lilly sashays out of the room, Angela states, "That one is different from the rest of your staff."

"Oh?" I scratch Colossus's apple-shaped head, and he closes his eyes in a blissed-out expression.

"She's attractive," Angela says. "Suspiciously so. And feisty—which I didn't think you could tolerate."

I scoff. "You're just feeling defensive and lashing out."

Angela originally bought the dog for herself. Then, after merely two weeks, she begged me to take him—and I couldn't say no. That's what she meant when she told Lilly that "life happens."

Angela sighs theatrically. "You're brutally honest, as usual. I wonder how *Lilly* feels about that."

Not this shit again. "Abraham Lincoln is revered for his honesty. Why am I always getting chided for mine?"

She snorts. "I bet if his wife ever asked him if a

dress made her look fat, even Honest Abe would've said no regardless of the truth. That's called a white lie and it's what makes our society function."

I sigh. "You lie enough for the both of us."

"That's not fair. I'm always honest with *you*."

I can't help but smile. "That there is the biggest lie of the day."

She rolls her eyes. "Well, here's a truth: that Lilly seems like trouble."

"On that, we agree," I say. "But as you know, I don't have a lot of time, so how about we talk about the dumb dog?"

"Don't listen to him," she croons at Colossus. "You're a genius."

"Yeah. A genius who ate half a roll of toilet paper the other day."

"Daddy and I love you," Angela continues in the same babytalk. "If he doesn't tell you that, it's because he's a big grump who doesn't even say it to me."

"According to his papers, his 'daddy' was a best-in-show winner named Toby," I snap.

"No," Angela says. "That was just the sperm donor."

How is it that even after years of arguing with her, I still haven't learned that it's a waste of time? I change the topic. "In any case, the dog is doing well. Lilly has big plans for his training."

The gambit works, and the conversation pivots to all things Colossus. When she's up to speed, I ask her how she's liking the Hamptons—her current stop on her ever-busy itinerary.

"It's surprisingly like your Palm Beach." She wrinkles her nose. "Everyone makes their hedges taller than their neighbors'."

"That reminds me," I say. "I should get forty-foot hedges to surround *my* estate."

She rolls her eyes. "It's secluded as is. You don't need the privacy."

I shrug. "If there's a contest on hedge heights, I intend to win."

"First the car collection, now this," Angela says. "Someone might think you're trying to compensate for something."

"Seriously?"

"Sorry," Angela says sheepishly. "That was below the belt."

"I'm hanging up now."

"Wait," she says. "Have you spoken to your parents today?"

"No," I say. "I haven't spoken to *our* parents."

"Then this will be a surprise," she says triumphantly. "I'm coming for a visit."

I frown. "With Champ?"

"Of course."

Fuck. I know it's a typical thing for a brother to disapprove of anyone his sister dates, but in this case, I'm justified because Champ is the epitome of a douche. "But what about his dog allergy?" I demand.

Angela met Champ a few days after she got Colossus, and it didn't take long for them to decide to go globetrotting together—without a dog.

"We'll stay at a hotel," she says. "And when we visit, your Lilly can keep the dog out of Champ's way. Also, he will take some antihistamines."

I blow out an exasperated breath. I thought one bonus of having this dog was that I wouldn't have to be in the same space as Champ ever again.

"You don't like it when *I* poopoo on the people you date," Angela says.

"Which you do," I say. "Every single time."

She shrugs. "It's not my fault you're a magnet for gold-digging trash."

I pointedly look at my watch. "We're out of time."

It's not even an excuse. It's dinnertime for me and Colossus, and I haven't delegated that task to Lilly just yet.

Angela pouts. "You just don't want to have a conversation about your love life. Or lack thereof."

Tapping at the clockface, I wave her goodbye.

"How long has it been?" she asks stubbornly. "A year. Two?"

I reply by hanging up. The last thing I need is to be told that I need a good woman in my life—whatever that means.

Colossus looks down and whines.

I set him on the floor. "You hungry?"

We both know the question is rhetorical. The puppy bolts out of the room like he's being attacked by bees, then torpedoes in the direction of the kitchen.

Even walking fast, I can barely keep up with him.

When I get to the kitchen, I slow down.

There's always a risk I might catch someone chewing in there, like the time I walked in on the chef tasting his alfredo sauce, or the time I—

And there it is.

Her back to me, Lilly is sitting on a barstool with a fork in her hand, a piece of gnocchi speared on it. She has headphones on, so she doesn't notice me or the dog.

Before I can look away, she sticks the fork into her mouth and begins chewing.

I wince, expecting the usual flood of adrenaline and wave of disgust.

None of it comes.

What the fuck? Until now, the only creature whose eating I could tolerate was the dog—and I figured it was because a) he mostly swallows without chewing, and b) he finishes his food in a nanosecond.

In morbid fascination, I wait until she spears another gnocchi.

Was that a moan?

Yep.

She's *really* enjoying her meal.

And once again, I feel nothing.

Well, if I'm honest, my heart rate does go up, but it's not due to the usual reasons. It's her moaning. I never realized that eating with zest could sound so seductive.

Hmm. Is that why I'm seemingly immune to her chewing? Is this the famous "suspension bridge effect" from psychology, where men find women more attractive after receiving an adrenaline surge from walking over a bridge? Yeah. It must be that. Some wires have gotten crossed, and my body thinks I'm turned on instead of feeling the usual fight-or-flight response.

Lilly greedily slurps her drink through a straw.

Normally, I'd be climbing the walls by now, yet I'm fine... or more accurately, turned on *more.*

I feel paws tapping my shin.

Ah.

Right.

The dog is reminding me why I'm here.

I walk over to the fridge and get the soy sauce dish that we use as a doggie plate. The chef has outdone himself, as usual, setting up all the morsels in a pretty way.

Out of the corner of my eye, I see Lilly take off her headphones.

"Hey," she says. "Is he about to eat?"

I set the bowl down in answer.

Channeling the Flash, Colossus whooshes over and devours the whole meal in an eyeblink. Even though I've seen this before, I shake my head. Why do I make the chef waste his time to make the dog's food look so presentable?

Lilly's eyes widen so much they look proportional to her eyebrows... at least for the moment. "I've seen dogs eat fast, but this may be a Guinness world record."

The stupidest thing happens next. My lungs expand with pride, as though fast eating is an accomplishment on par with solving a quadratic equation, calculating a derivative, or programming a VCR. "It's *too* quick," I grumble. "Sometimes he's so fast he makes himself sick."

She nods knowingly. "There are products on the market that can slow him down."

"Oh?"

She pulls out her phone, does a search, and shows me something that looks like a blue honeycomb. "It's called a lick mat," she says. "If you mash up his food or run it through a blender, you can smear in on that thing, and he'll have to take his time licking it off."

"I thought you followed the golden rule," I say. "Licking your food sounds frustrating."

Then again, the next time someone insists on having a lunch meeting with me, this could be the way I make them eat, as it would eliminate all chewing sounds.

She bristles. "Obviously, you can't always go by how a human might feel about something. We don't sniff butts, for example, but dogs love it."

"Are you saying I need to provide my dog with butts to sniff?"

"No," she says. "I mean, yes, for socialization, you should have him meet other dogs, but I was trying to say that dogs find licking very soothing."

Making a mental note to come back to this socialization business, I take out my own phone and buy a few different kinds of lick mats to test out.

"Great," she says when I tell her what I've done. "I'll work with Bob on slowing the puppy down once they arrive."

I cringe. "Can you at least call him Chef?"

She rolls her eyes but says, "Fine."

A compromise? Mercury must be in retrograde.

"Anyway." I walk over to the oven where my food is being kept warm. "I'll let you enjoy your meal."

"Ah. Right." She grabs her plate with a jerky motion. "I was warned not to eat in your august presence."

"Who warned you?" I demand. My staff shouldn't be talking about this.

She takes a step back. "No one."

I point at the ceiling. "There's a surveillance camera up there, so I *could* find out for myself." It's a bluff, at least regarding my looking at the footage personally—it might include people chewing. But I *could* have someone from security comb through it if I felt like it.

"Then check your fucking camera," she grits out. "Just leave me out of it."

Colossus whines.

Fuck.

I take a deep breath and prepare to deescalate. "It's fine that they told you. You would have found out sooner or later—and nondisclosure is part of the contract you signed."

"It is?"

"Yes." And a good thing too, as what I'm about to tell her I rarely, if ever, share with people.

She stares at me, intrigued. "So… what is it I'm not to disclose?"

I take another breath. "I have misophonia."

CHAPTER 13
LILLY

feel like an ass that no dog would ever want to sniff. Jerk or not, this guy has a real condition, and here I am, mocking him about it.

Misunderstanding my silence, he says, "Misophonia is when someone has negative responses to certain trigger sounds. Think nails on chalkboard. In my case, it's chewing and slurping." He winces as he says the last bit.

"I know that," I say. "I took a DNA test, and one of the reports explained what it is and told me I'm unlikely to have it."

He nods. "TENM2 is the gene involved. I haven't done that test, as I'm not sure what the point of such a report would be. If you have what I have, you know it."

Yep. Feeling worse by the second. How does he go on dates with that hot woman from the video if he can't tolerate the sounds of people eating? How does he attend holiday dinners with his family? Or go to business lunches?

"I'm sorry," I mutter.

He shrugs. "It's not your fault."

"I meant, I'm sorry for giving you shit about it. Also, I'm sorry I started eating here in the kitchen when I knew it was your dinnertime. I wasn't thinking."

Or maybe a part of me wanted to piss him off. Or see him—but I'm not going to psychoanalyze myself right now.

He darts a glance at my plate. "To be honest, for some strange reason, seeing you eat didn't trigger anything."

Huh. "Has that happened before?"

He shakes his head. "The dog's eating doesn't bother me, but that's about it."

Should I feel special, or did he just compare me to a dog? "Well," I say. "If you want to eat together, I'd be okay with that."

Wait. What am I saying? What am I going to do if he takes me up on this? But of course, he wouldn't. Spending time with me is the last thing he'd—

"Okay," he says without missing a beat.

"Okay?"

He sets his plate near mine on the bar. "Let's try this. If I get irritable or—"

"You're always irritable."

He blows out a breath. "Look who's talking."

"Sorry," I say. "Go on."

"If I *feel* symptoms, I'll up and leave."

"All right." Who knew that instead of yelling at my nemesis, I'd end up having dinner with him?

I take my seat, put food in my mouth, and chew self-consciously. He seems to be okay, but I ask, "How do you feel?"

"Great," he says.

Dare I ask if it's thanks to my company?

"I've always been jealous of people who can eat during work meetings," he continues. "Meals are my least productive times of day—while I'm awake, anyway."

So, there you have it. It's not my company he's enjoying—the workaholic in him just loves the opportunity to multitask. A better question is: why does this bother me so much? I don't know, but my words sound stiff as I ask, "Is there anything related to training that you wanted to discuss?"

"Socialization," he says. "You mentioned it earlier. I want more details."

Done with his demand, he fills his mouth with gnocchi—and damn, something about the way he chews makes me hungrier.

"Let me explain why it's important first," I say. "Properly socialized dogs have less anxiety and therefore lead happier lives. They are also more pleasant to be around because they don't react negatively when they encounter certain situations."

He swallows his food. "You'll socialize him then. What does it entail?"

I smile at Colossus—who's sitting and looking up at

us, clearly begging for food. "Not sure if this counts as socialization, but he needs to be comfortable with as many new smells, sounds, sights, and textures as possible." We don't want him to be like Roach, who refused to step on sand because of my oversight in this area.

Bruce nods, urging me to go on.

"He also needs to be introduced to lots of people, one at a time at first, then in groups. Since he loves food, these people can give him treats, so he forms positive associations."

"Okay," Bruce says, but he looks less pleased about this—probably because he's a misanthrope and what I've just described involves having people around.

"These people need to be as varied as possible," I say. "Think different fitness levels, ages, ethnic backgrounds, disabilities, and even different types of clothing. If you don't expose Colossus to diversity, you could end up with a dog who barks at people in wheelchairs, or at kids, or at anyone who wears sunglasses while holding an umbrella."

"Makes sense," he says. "Do these people need to come to the house?"

I shake my head. "The most natural thing would be to meet them outside, which is neutral territory. But this being a private estate, I'm not sure if—"

"I'll make some arrangements," he cuts in. "What else?"

"Same idea when it comes to animals," I say. "You don't want him stressed out if he meets another dog, or a cat, or a squirrel."

He scratches his chin. "I'll see what I can do."

"That's the gist of it." I finish the rest of my food and look for his reaction to my chewing.

Nothing.

I put down my fork. "Anything else?"

He glances at Colossus, who's begging for all he's worth. "I want him to make it through the night without an accident."

I fight the urge to toss the little beggar a treat. "Until his bladder is mature, he has to be walked at night."

"You'll do it then," Bruce declares.

"I was planning on it," I say. "Where does he currently sleep?"

Bruce eats another morsel, then says, "In my bedroom."

In. His. Bedroom? But that would mean—

Never mind that, actually. Why is the bigger mystery. Also, how come—

"The damn dog whines if I don't let him in there," Bruce says defensively, answering one of my million questions.

To give myself a chance to process this, I take my plate to the sink, rinse it, and then stick it in the dishwasher.

"Don't do that next time," Bruce says. "Mrs. Campbell will clean up."

I roll my eyes. "I was raised to clean up after myself."

He scoffs. "Why use the dishwasher then?"

"How the hell am I going to walk him at night if he's in your bedroom?" I blurt.

Bruce's eyebrows snap together. "How about you set an alarm, walk over, and take the dog out?"

"From your *bedroom*," I say, overenunciating the last word.

Leave it to a man to take *this* long to realize the problem with this scenario, but judging by the "oh" his lips form, I think he's finally got it.

"There will be nothing inappropriate," he says.

He doesn't have to sound *that* certain—like I'm the most unfuckable woman he's ever met.

"Do you sleep naked?" I demand—and promptly blush.

He sighs. "I don't *have* to."

Oh, the images. The salacious, mouthwatering images. "Yeah. No nakedness." Even though I'm already regretting the demand.

"Anything else?" he asks. "What side should I sleep on?"

Not dignifying that with a reply, I eye the two big cups on the counter that are filled with a thick liquid—half of it white and the other red.

"That's the panna cotta," Bruce says when he notices where I'm looking. "If you like it, you can have mine."

Is this him being nice?

I grab a spoon, make sure I capture both colors, then stick the gooey goodness into my mouth.

Wow. So good.

The dog gives me a pleading look.

Give that to me. It looks like a liquid cookie. I'll do anything—even let you brush my teeth afterward.

I shake my head. There are grapes in the red part of this dish, and those are toxic to dogs.

Looking at Bruce instead of the puppy, I take another spoonful, and this time, I inadvertently suck the yumminess from the spoon with too much ardor, which results in a slurping sound, albeit a very faint one.

Bruce flinches like he's been struck and leaps to his feet, fists clenched.

Colossus tucks his tail between his legs and whines pitifully.

"I'm *so* sorry," I mutter and push the rest of the dessert as far away from me as I can. "That was an accident." One I should strive to avoid while in his company, for the same reasons as belching, picking my nose, and farting.

Bruce closes his eyes, takes in a deep breath, and lets it out meditatively. "You weren't testing me?"

"No." I point at my burning cheeks. "Does it help that I'm embarrassed?"

He sits back down and takes another calming breath. "Fewer and fewer people consider it rude to slurp at the table. Next thing you know, we'll turn into Japan."

I let my eyebrow ask the obvious question.

"The Japanese consider it acceptable—and maybe desirable—to slurp things like ramen, soba, and udon."

He shudders. "They also sip soup straight out of the bowl."

"I take it you're not going there anytime soon?"

"Never again," he says. "For good measure, I avoid traveling to Asia in general—and during teleconferences, I make it a rule not to allow eating of any kind."

"I understand if you never want to eat with me again," I say. "Though, if you'd like, I could simply forgo liquid desserts and soups while I'm in your employ."

Why am I still talking? What makes me presume he'd want to eat with me—the help—again? Nor do I want that, not really, not if—

"No milkshakes either," he says. "And if you have a drink, use a straw—but stop about three quarters of the way through, and then get a refill or pour it out."

"What about raw oysters?" I ask.

He wrinkles his nose. "After giving me a lecture about norovirus, hepatitis A, *and* salmonella, the chef has been cooking oysters."

"The horror," I say. "Rich people without raw oysters? Next thing you know, he'll ban caviar."

"Caviar is not raw. It's salted, and therefore on the menu from time to time," Bruce says with a straight face. "But the chef *is* against sashimi—even if someone were to catch and kill the fish right in front of him."

I chuckle. "Do *you* even trust sashimi—it being from Japan and all?"

Before he can reply, there's a loud feminine gasp from behind me.

Oh, shit. Is that the girlfriend from the video call?

No.

It's Prudence. She's staring at the panna cotta that I started as though it were an explosive device, and I now know why.

"I think I'd better walk Colossus," I say sheepishly. The last thing I want is to get into the reasons why I broke the biggest household taboo on my first day.

Bruce's icy demeanor returns—which makes me realize it was missing toward the end of our conversation.

"Come," I tell the puppy.

He doesn't move.

Ah. Right. There's food nearby.

"Here." I take out a piece of cookie.

Oh, boy. I have the furry one's eerily focused attention now.

Give it. Give it. You can't pull that out and not share. I'll die of starvation right here, right now, I swear.

"You can have this once you get your harness on," I singsong.

I'm not sure if he understands, but he follows me to the garage and waits patiently while I put on his accoutrements.

"Good boy." I give him the treat, and he nearly bites my fingers as he greedily devours it.

"You'll have to learn how to do that more politely," I say and put on my goofy headgear.

———

When we return to the mansion, Colossus dashes away as soon as he's free—and I chase him all the way to the library, just like the last time.

Bruce is there, reading again, only this time I manage to spot the name of his book, which prompts me to excitedly exclaim, "You're reading *The Witcher*?"

Bruce snaps the book closed with irritation—and I recall him saying he only allows himself to read for "a few precious minutes per day."

"Yes," he says, voice less prickly than I expected. "*The Witcher* is my favorite book series."

"Wow," is all I can say.

Bruce picks up the puppy at his feet and puts him on his lap. "Are you a fan of Andrzej Sapkowski?"

I frown. "Who?"

With an eyeroll, Bruce points at the book cover.

I feel stupid, since of course, I should have figured he's talking about the book's author. "If he had anything to do with my favorite video game of all time, then yes, I'm a fan."

"What game?" Bruce scratches Colossus behind his ear, causing the little furball to close his eyes in bliss.

I gape at him. "You're kidding, right?"

Bruce shakes his head.

"You're a fan of the books about the Witcher, yet you've never played the games?"

He sighs. "Narrow it down for me. Are we talking card games, board games, or—"

"Video games," I say. "Hear of those?"

He cringes. "Yeah. They're what your generation replaced books with."

"You're not seventy. We're the same generation," I say. "The first ever video game was created in 1958. That's far in the past, even for a relic such as you."

"Fine," he says. "You like *The Witcher* video games."

"Specifically, *The Witcher 3*. Or more specifically, the best game of the 2010s. Yes, I was already alive back then."

He shrugs. "Never heard of it."

CHAPTER 14
BRUCE

"Did you live under a rock?" she asks, and her eyebrows grow so animated I half expect them to join the conversation.

I stare her down—which is easier now because when I'm sitting and she's standing, our eyes are almost level. "This, coming from the person who didn't know the name of the author of her 'favorite game.'"

With a huff, she pulls out her phone and does a search. "No," she says. "The books did come first, but the author simply sold the rights to the game developer. He didn't write anything for them after."

"There you go," I say. "There's no way those games could be anywhere as good as the books."

Her eyes go slitty. "*The Witcher 3* is a masterpiece."

"If you say so."

She turns on her heel. "I'll prove it to you."

Before I can reply, she stomps off somewhere.

I stare at Colossus. "How is she going to prove that to me?"

The puppy just wags his tail. He likes being in my lap in the evenings and doesn't care for much else.

Reaching for my book, I resume reading until I hear the pitter-patter of tiny feet, followed by an angry throat clearing.

"Yes?" I put the book away for what feels like the hundredth time.

She thrusts something into my hands—a gizmo that looks like a large smartphone with a video game controller attached on each side. "Play *this*, and I dare you to tell me it's not the best thing ever."

I check out the screen, where I see a computer-generated likeness of Geralt, a.k.a. the Witcher, standing next to a horse.

"They've got the hair right," I say. "And there're two swords. I assume the horse's name is Roach."

"There are also sexy sorceresses," she says so enticingly that it reverberates in my cock.

"Triss and Yennefer?" I can't help but ask.

Looking like the proverbial cat who ate the canary, she asks, "Does that mean you'll play?"

I hand her my book. "Only if you read this."

She takes the book between her thumb and index finger like it might bite. "It's been a while since I've read a book."

I tsk-tsk. "All the more reason to read something *now*, before your brain permanently atrophies—like those of the rest of your short-attention-spanned cohorts."

"Says the ancient," she says sarcastically, then riffles through the pages, looking uncertain.

"Look," I say. "The last time I played a video game was back in high school."

She becomes a lot more animated at this. "What was the game?

"*Super Mario Sunshine.*"

"GameCube?" she asks excitedly.

"I think so. I even still have the thing somewhere in storage."

Her eyes gleam. "I had the GameCube, and that game was my favorite when I was in grade school."

"Grade school?" If she wanted to make me feel like an antique, mission accomplished.

"Yep." She points at the device in my hands. "That's a Nintendo console as well."

I turn the gizmo over and read the back of it. "Nintendo Switch?"

"You've never heard of it?" She shakes her head. "You really *do* live under a rock."

I sigh. "If being a grown adult is the same thing as living under a rock, then I'm guilty as charged."

"I'm an adult." As if unaware of the concept of irony, she accompanies the statement with a stomp of her little foot.

"Will you read the book or not?" I hand her the game console back since I'm confident she'll go for the "not" option.

She grasps the book tighter. "I'll only commit to finishing this if you swear that you'll beat the whole game."

"Deal."

She grins triumphantly. "You know it's about a hundred hours, right?"

"What?" I nearly drop the stupid console. "You'll be done with the book in a tenth of that time."

"So… you're welshing already?" She hands the book to me.

"No. It might have taken *you* that long to beat the game, but I figure if I focus, I can do it faster."

She grins. "Good luck."

"I don't need luck."

Her grin widens. "That's the spirit. Oh, and you can play on 'easy' if that's what you need."

"That's why books are better," I say pointedly. "No shortcuts."

She opens her mouth to make some sort of a retort, but Mrs. Campbell interrupts us once again. This time, she's carrying a tray with my nightly digestif.

"Well," Lilly says. "I'd better go."

"Do you remember where your room is?" I ask.

"Yes," she says, but doesn't sound too sure.

I take my drink from Mrs. Campbell. "Can you show her where it is, as well as Colossus's sleeping arrangements?"

"Of course," Mrs. Campbell says.

"Have fun," Lilly says, nodding at the video game in my hand.

I wait for them to leave before I navigate my way to the "New Game" screen.

A part of me is actually excited, but that could very well be the aftermath of having Lilly in my presence. Either way, I never put off something for later if it can be done immediately, which means now is as good of a time as any to acquaint myself with the silicon version of the Witcher.

This will take my reading time slot—which means I have mere minutes before I have to get back to work.

CHAPTER 15
LILLY

As Prudence takes me from my room to Bruce's bedroom, I memorize the path so that I will be able to retrace my steps while I'm sleepy.

"Be careful when you approach the dog," Prudence says as she opens the biggest set of doors I've seen in this mansion—and maybe ever. "He can get noisy if startled."

"That makes sense. I can get noisy if startled too."

Smiling, she gestures for me to enter. I step inside and ogle my surroundings.

Bruce's bedroom is the size of many people's houses, yet the only furniture is a huge fancy bed—and a tiny replica of the same bed a few feet away.

"That is the cutest thing I've ever seen," I say. "But why?"

"Why what, dear?" Prudence asks.

I point at the miniature. "Why does the dog's bed look just like Bruce's?"

She turns furtively to make sure we're alone. "I'm not sure," she says in a low voice. "I think the puppy would beg to sleep in Mr. Roxford's bed, and I believe that he thought the issue was that the doggie bed wasn't comfortable, so he had an exact replica of his own bed commissioned."

"Did it help?" I whisper back.

"Maybe. Or maybe the little one got used to sleeping separately by then—it's hard to be sure."

I thank her for showing me around and make my way back to my room.

Since my stuff is still mostly packed, I work on settling in for a bit, but once again, the deluge of impending decisions hampers my progress.

I also realize that I didn't bring anything like a hamper for my laundry, so I'll have to ask Prudence for one. For now, my dirty clothes can go into a pile on the floor.

Yawning, I test out my bathroom and learn that the shower can give amazing massages and the floor tiles are luxuriously warm when you step on them with bare feet.

The top point-zero-zero-one percent live well, I have to say. I'd better not get too used to it.

After the shower, I get into bed, where I discover that my sheets are made of silk—or something else heavenly.

As I close my eyes, my mind whirls—especially around the fact that I started this morning on a mission to yell at the personification of evil and ended the day in his bed.

Or at least a bed he owns.

Unbidden, my parents' situation comes to the forefront of my mind. Just before I was born, they bought their first house. It was almost paid off, but then my dad needed surgery and my parents refinanced to pay the medical bills. Dad's health didn't allow him to return to work, and Mom lost her job because she had to care for him. I tried to help them as much as I could, but my job barely covered my own bills. No one at Bruce's bank gave a shit about our story, though, and my parents lost the house.

A squeezing pain invades my chest again, thinking of all those memories that we'll never get to relive—not even if I can help my parents buy another house with the money I'm going to earn here.

Because of Bruce, my childhood home is gone for good.

Grr.

There's no way I'll fall asleep with this shit on my mind.

Opening my eyes, I grab *The Witcher* and begin reading.

Huh. It's surprisingly good, even for someone who hasn't picked up a book in a while. Maybe it's because it's a collection of short stories and thus doesn't require the long attention span necessary for a novel.

Before I know it, I'm done with the first story. Blinking, I check the clock—and smack myself on the head. I have to wake up to walk the dog in the middle of the night, so if I want to get decent rest prior to that, I should be asleep right now.

Setting an alarm, I close my eyes again, but sleep eludes me—this time, because I'm dreading walking into Bruce's room in a few hours.

All right.

By the time I finish the second story, I have to grudgingly admit that the book is better than the game, at least insofar as you can compare such different things. The book version of Geralt is cooler, more tormented, more morally gray, and sexier—and this last bit is coming from someone who might've masturbated to the scene in the video game where he takes a bath.

Of course, it goes without saying that I would never, ever admit any of this to Bruce.

Damn it. I shouldn't think about Bruce—not if I want to get any sleeping done.

I tentatively close my eyes, and the moment when we almost kissed smashes into my mind.

Fine.

More reading.

And more, until I realize that it's time to walk the dog already.

Getting up, I put on some clothes and traverse the path to Bruce's bedroom.

Taking in a calming breath, I open the giant doors.

Wow. The darkness is absolute, as if it were the inside of a black hole. Usually, a room has some gizmo with an LED light shining, or moonlight seeping through the windows, or *something*.

Oh, well. I pull out my phone and use it as a flashlight to navigate to the tiny replica bed. When I'm halfway there, I see two tiny green lights shining—Colossus's eyes.

I smile and wave my phone at him, which must be a mistake because he starts barking loudly. Way too loudly for a creature his size.

Shit. This isn't good.

His barks now sound like a tiny wolf cub's howl—something that would be adorable if it weren't happening in the bedroom of my nemesis and employer in the middle of the night.

Crap. What do I do?

I'm so screwed.

"Alexa, bedroom lights on!" Bruce shouts over the barks, and I'm momentarily blinded.

Colossus's next bark is less howly, and then he quiets down.

Feeling like a guillotine is about to fall on my neck, I reluctantly face the big bed, squinting against the bright lights overhead—only to feel my jaw hit the floor.

Wearing nothing but slim-fitting briefs, Bruce is looming over me, every chiseled muscle in his powerful body tight with anger.

CHAPTER 16
LILLY

O r maybe it's not anger. Can you have an erection while angry? No idea, but that's an epic one under those briefs. So big I can't believe the underwear is able to contain it.

Being short, I've felt dwarfed by things before—but never by something that's technically smaller than I am. Yet somehow his cock has that effect.

How does Bruce have enough blood left in his body to function—and to flex all those muscles? He should've left his dog's name as Peanut and named his cock Colossus instead. Or Titan. Or—

"What is going on?" Bruce demands.

I take a step back. "I'm here for Titan. I mean, Colossus." It takes all my willpower to drag my eyes upward to Bruce's face instead of staring at his Titan.

"Alexa, dim bedroom lights," Bruce growls.

The brightness subsides.

Seeing the murderous expression in Bruce's icy

eyes, I take another step back and mutter, "I'm sorry. Seems like Colossus got startled."

Bruce angrily strides over to a nearby closet and wraps himself in a robe.

The disappointment I feel is almost proportional to Titan—which is obviously stupid.

"I thought you were a professional," Bruce says grimly.

"What do you mean?" I demand. It's like the man has the superpower of raising my hackles.

"I mean that a dog trainer should be able to come get her charge without having him go berserk with stress."

I hate him all the more because he's right. "I'm sorry. Next time, I'll crack open the door and use a cookie to lure him out."

In fact, I probably would've thought about this earlier if I weren't so sleepy.

Bruce shakes his head. "His bed is moving to *your* room."

"Fine," I say. "Can we go now?"

He waves me off imperiously. "Just make sure to wear protection. Owls hunt at night."

I roll my eyes and turn to face Colossus.

The little fur ball wags his tail, all earlier barking forgotten.

"Come," I say.

He trots over to me, and I lead him to the garage to gear up.

Outside, the night air smells wonderful, and the full

moon illuminates the estate beautifully, making this walk a joy despite the late hour. Colossus does his business pretty quickly—no doubt eager to return to bed. I pick him up and carry him to Bruce's bedroom, where I open the doors as carefully as I can.

Hmm.

There's a light inside.

I gingerly step in, only to gape at the source.

Bruce is playing my Switch… in bed.

"*The Witcher 3?*" I blurt.

He grunts in the affirmative.

"Do you like it so far?"

He gives another grunt.

I guess he didn't want to be awakened again, so he decided to kill the time by gaming—which is exactly what I would have done.

Without saying another word, I deposit Colossus and skedaddle.

Once in my own room, I shamelessly head for my box of sex toys, as I can see only one way to get any shuteye at this point: a visit to my bat cave.

No. Bat cave makes me think of Batman, and his name is Bruce—and that's not who I want in my head for this. I'd better think about someone else, like the computer-generated Witcher.

Yeah.

That's the ticket. With this in mind, I proceed to ménage à moi.

CHAPTER 17
BRUCE

Why is this fucking game so fucking addictive?

Forcing myself to power down the console, I lie on my back and think about what happened earlier.

One second, I was inside Lilly in a dream; the next, there she was.

Why the hell did I have that dream? And why did she look so magnificent standing there when I woke up?

It must've been that stupid suspension bridge effect messing with my mind again. The barking startled me awake, and then there she was. That must be it because I don't like any other explanations for the way my body reacted.

Turning onto my left side, I grasp my pillow and hope for sleep.

Nope.

Maybe I'll have better luck on the right side?

It's even worse.

After tossing and turning for what feels like an hour, I decide that it's time for one of two home remedies that help me sleep: a snack or jerking off.

A snack seems like the better option as it's not likely to make me think of Lilly again—which would be counterproductive if the goal is to clear her from my mind.

Tossing on my robe, I head for the fridge. I'm not surprised when I hear the pitter-patter of small, fluffy feet behind me. Colossus never misses a chance to go to the kitchen—not since he's figured out that that's where his treats reside.

As we approach the kitchen, he runs ahead of me, which is odd.

When I enter, I understand.

It's Lilly. She's standing with her back to us.

Without realizing what I'm doing, I rub my eyes, feeling like I'm in a wet dream again.

Lilly is wearing some sort of a sleep romper that consists of a thin strappy top and tiny shorts—as in, most of her back, arms, and shoulders are deliciously bare, as are her smooth, sexy legs.

My robe tents. Of fucking course. Coming here was a *big* mistake.

Maybe I can back away before—

Colossus dashes toward her, and when he gets to the fridge, he looks up and whines.

Odd. He doesn't usually do that.

"I'm sorry," she says to him, sounding very guilty. "I was just curious."

What is she talking about?

No. I don't care. It's better if I leave.

I take a soft step back, but she must hear it, or feel the air vibrate from my fucking hard-on—because she turns.

Fuck.

If I thought her outfit was sexy from the back, it pretty much makes my balls turn blue from the front.

Since I'm busted, I make sure the table is between her eyesight and my crotch, then employ the best defense in such a situation—offense. "What are you doing here?"

She shoots the dog a guilty glance. "I couldn't sleep, so I came here for a bite to eat. When I saw *his* food in the fridge, I got curious, so I—"

"You're eating dog food?" I ask incredulously.

She stashes the bowl she's been holding back into the fridge. "It's made by a private chef and from human-grade ingredients. I just wanted to taste it."

The dog whines louder—a sound that tugs at something in my chest and forces me to stride over to the fridge and snatch the bowl in question. With a loud thud, I put it on the floor.

As usual, the puppy attacks the meal as if it's his first one after a year-long fast.

"That's a mistake," Lilly mutters under her breath.

I look down at her—and regret it instantly. Her

romper is loose at the bodice and she's not wearing a bra, so I get an eyeful of her deliciously perky little breasts, and even spot a pale pink nipple that is hard as a pebble —no doubt from the cold emanating out of the fridge.

Why the fuck did I get so close to her? For such a tiny creature, she exudes a powerful gravity field that draws me in—but giving in would be the worst idea ever.

"How was that a mistake?" I ask, figuring more defense is my best move at this juncture.

She lifts her adorable chin. "Colossus whined, and you fed him right afterward. That's positive reinforcement. Now he's much more likely to do that again the next time he wants to get his way."

Fuck. She's right. "Should I take it away?"

She glances down. "Too late."

Yep. He's all done—and that was his whole breakfast.

"That's the shelf with human snacks." I point at the section of the fridge that was my own destination.

Did she just look at the protrusion in my robe?

Shit. I forgot about that.

Thinking unsexy thoughts is futile, so I misdirect her attention by reaching for food. The problem is, at that exact moment, she reaches for the same item—and our fingers brush.

If my cock had a voice, he'd be roaring in frustration.

Gasping, she grabs a spinach artichoke twist and

stuffs it into her mouth, as if I were going to steal it from her.

Once again, my reaction is sexual instead of the usual fight-or-flight I get when I see people eating—but in my defense, what else can you expect when she's wrapping her lips over such a phallic-looking object?

"Does my eating bother you?" she asks after she swallows. "Please tell me if it's like the panna cotta."

"I'll tell you," I say and grab one of the avocado deviled eggs. Like her, I swallow it almost without chewing.

"Good," she says and stares at my lips intently. Her voice has a peculiarly breathy quality that makes my cock twitch.

Damn it. I need to step away. Now. But for some reason, my feet refuse to move. We stare at each other, barely a foot of space separating us, and my heartbeat picks up as the moment stretches—the way I ache for her pussy to stretch around my cock.

No, what am I thinking? I need to stop this. Right now. *Move, feet, move back now.* But they disobey, taking the tiniest step forward, and I hear her breath hitch in her throat, see her eyes widen as she realizes what's happening. And then... Oh, fuck, somehow I'm kissing those soft, tempting lips, and she—holy fuck—is kissing me back. Her delicate arms wrap around my neck, and she all but climbs me like a baby koala would a prime eucalyptus tree—and it's the hottest thing I've ever experienced.

A sudden bark wrenches me out of the kiss.

I pull away just as Lilly leaps backward, like she's been burned.

For a dog trainer, she sure is skittish of barking.

The source of the bark is obviously the dog, but he's not distressed, as I initially assumed. He's actually looking up at us excitedly and wagging his tail for all he's worth. My guess is, he thought the kiss was something fun and wanted to get in on it.

Lilly and I stare at each other, our breaths uneven, and then we say in perfect unison, "That was a mistake."

I frown immediately, some of the heat leaving my body. I know why I'd say that, but why would she? I'm the employer here, not the other way around, and she's not the one—

"A mistake?" Lilly hisses, her eyes turning slitty, like those of a fox.

Before I can retort, she turns on her heel and dashes away.

I look down at the puppy to see if he understands what's just happened.

Doubtful. He stares after Lilly's disappearing back disappointedly.

I take a deep breath and let it out slowly, then pick up the dog to calm myself further. It works—it's amazing what a little ball of fur can do for one's state of mind. He's like a Xanax that eats and poops.

Doing my best not to think about that kiss, I carry him back to my bedroom and place him in his bed before I dive into mine. Closing my eyes, I try to sleep, but without the dog distracting me, the kiss comes to the forefront of my mind. The kiss and its aftermath. And the more I dwell on the latter, the angrier I get.

Why would she say it was a mistake? If *Forbes* is to be believed, I'm a catch and certainly not someone you treat like a foot fungus.

Maybe she's a socialist, or some other "ist" that hates the wealthy?

I have no idea, but I know this much: something like that kiss must never, ever happen again.

CHAPTER 18
LILLY

A mistake?

How dare he say that kissing me was a mistake? He wasn't the one kissing his nemesis. He wasn't the one kissing a man who seems to already have a girlfriend... or even a wife.

I dive angrily into my bed and smack the pillow, wishing it were his face.

The thing that pisses me off the most is the fact that the kiss was off-the-charts amazing.

The best I've ever had.

Better than I could imagine a kiss ever being.

Great. Now I'm even hornier.

Oh well, there's no avoiding it. Time to angrily masturbate myself to sleep.

———

When I come to the kitchen for breakfast, luck isn't on my side. Bruce—whom I was hoping to avoid—is here, and he's just starting on his Eggs Benedict.

"Morning," he says. "I'm glad you're here. I want to discuss your plans for the day."

Is that how he wants to play it? Pretend that nothing happened?

Fine. I'm glad, actually. The last thing I want is to relive that humiliation.

"Morning," I say with fake cheerfulness. "Colossus and I will work on 'sit.'"

Upon hearing his name, Colossus leaves his place by Bruce's feet and runs over to me, tail wagging.

"Hi," I croon. "You miss me?"

As if in answer, Colossus plops on his back, exposing how lacking his belly is of fur.

Please, please, I want a belly rub. And a cookie. Maybe together?

Crouching, I gladly perform my belly-related duties, then grab my own Eggs Benedict and occupy a chair near Bruce.

"We're also going to walk," I continue. "And I'm going to teach him how to take a treat out of my hand politely."

Bruce nods approvingly, and I tell him what else I'm planning for today, time permitting.

As I talk, I watch Bruce for signs that my eating is bothering him, but he seems fine. Why does this make me feel special—especially after last night's fiasco?

"Are you a socialist?" Bruce suddenly asks.

I nearly choke on my next bite. "A socialist?"

He points at me with his fork. "A socialist is someone who thinks that things like production and distribution should be handled by the government rather than private corporations."

"I know *what* it is," I grit out.

"So you admit you are one?" he demands. "Don't worry. It won't disqualify you from working with Colossus."

I glance at the dog with a smirk. "Are you sure? What if I teach him 'hardworking Chihuahuas of the world, unite!'?"

"Now you're thinking communist," he says. "Tell me you aren't one of those."

"I don't think I am." I angrily cut my meal into little pieces. "I *do* think people like you have too much money."

He rolls his eyes. "That's called jealous-ism."

He thinks this is a joking matter? Not fully meaning to, I blurt out, "If someone falls on hard times, I think it's unfair for your bank to take their home. If that makes me a socialist, so be it."

"That *is* a shitty scenario," he says solemnly. "Which is why, at *my* bank, I've implemented a deferment program for qualified people, as well as forbearance."

"A what?" And why didn't my parents know about it?

"Forbearance is when someone is given some time without having to pay the mortgage, but the interest accrues. Deferment is similar, but interest free."

"Still." I fork some egg and bring it to my mouth. "Even your angel of a bank would eventually kick them out." As I chew, I mentally dare him to deny this.

He shrugs. "It's unfortunate, but it's not like we have much choice. If people didn't pay their mortgages, we'd go out of business—and how would new people get mortgages then?"

"And there you have it," I say. "Money is all that matters, not people's lives."

He exhales a frustrated breath. "Banks aren't putting guns to people's heads to force them to buy a house. There's aways renting, but folks want to own because they hope that the price of their home will grow—as in, they too want to make money in some distant future."

I'm so upset I forget to chew the next bite carefully, but he doesn't seem to notice.

"Is it wrong to want financial security when you're older?" I demand.

"Not at all. But guess what? You need banks for—"

Someone drops a fork, loudly.

It's Bob, the chef. He's staring at me eating with a horrified expression.

"I think that's my cue to leave," I say to no one in particular.

Shoving the rest of my egg into my mouth, I tempt Colossus with a cookie crumb to go for a walk.

Behind me, I hear Bruce explain to Bob that I'm the exception to his "eat alone rule"—which triggers that stupid feeling of specialness. But by the time I have the mohawk contraption on my head, I don't feel special anymore, at least not the version of that word without sarcastic quotes around it.

As soon as we're outside, Colossus starts sniffing a nearby bush, then lifts his leg.

"Good boy," I say, but before I can give him a treat, he lifts his leg again, a couple of inches to the left from the first time. As soon as he is done, he sniffs his work and goes one more time.

"Wow," I say with a grin. "You really wanted to mark that."

The puppy looks up at me, head cocked.

Well, duh. I'm making a masterpiece out of pee—or as art critics shall call it: a masterpees.

I give him a treat for the good work, then walk down the road... only to halt in my tracks because an attractive woman dressed in business attire is walking toward us—in high heels, on gravel.

What the hell? This is a private estate, so what is she doing here? Is this another romantic interest of Bruce's?

"Hello," I say when we're near enough not to have to shout, even if shouting at her is a tempting proposition.

"Hi," she says cheerfully. "You must be Lilly."

"That's me," I say. "Who are you?"

"I'm Gertrude," she says. "I work for Mr. Roxford." She looks at Colossus. "He said the dog needs to learn to be social, and that I'd be the first 'stranger' the little guy is to meet."

Huh. "You're a banker?"

"I am, but anything for Mr. Roxford."

As in, when he says, "Jump," she jumps. Very interesting.

"Here." I toss her a cookie. "When we get close to you, give him that, speak as you would to a baby, and don't make sudden moves."

We keep walking.

As we get closer to the woman, Colossus becomes more hesitant—until he spots the cookie in her hands. Now he seems torn. He wants the treat, but it's being held by a stranger.

"Go on," I say to him soothingly. "She's a nice lady." Probably.

"Hi, little guy," she coos. "Come have some of this." She waves the cookie.

Decision seemingly made, Colossus bravely lifts his chin and takes a determined step toward the woman. Then another.

"Here." She hands him a piece of the treat.

Wagging his tail, he accepts the offer.

She does it again and tries to pet him—and he lets her.

Wow. He's a quick learner. By the time the cookie is almost gone, he seems to have accepted the woman as his new BFF.

"Thank you," I say when I deem the lesson complete. "I'll make sure Bruce knows you did a great job here."

She beams at the puppy, then at me before heading over to a car parked nearby.

As we resume the walk, I see another car pull over not far away, and this time, a man steps out of it.

Another banker?

Yep.

This guy is chattier than the woman was, so I learn what Bruce has done—he's recruited every local branch of his bank into the puppy socialization project.

"So, yeah," the man says in conclusion. "The money is great, this dog is adorable, and it's nice to have a chance to get noticed by the big boss."

I provide the guy with the treat and the same instructions I gave the woman, which leads to the encounter going a bit smoother this time.

Not surprisingly, another car pulls up as soon as we're done. The man in this one is wearing big sunglasses and—as it turns out—has a prosthetic arm.

This encounter goes even better, even though I only give this man a portion of the treat.

I'm beginning to think that Colossus is actually a friendly dog. He just needed to learn that about himself.

The next person is an older lady with dandelion-like blue hair. The one after that is a teenage boy with cornrows. With less and less cookie each time, Colossus makes friends with them, and with the people who come after.

I have to grudgingly give Bruce's bank some credit —there is a great diversity of people working there… at least in the local branches.

"Ready to go back?" I ask the pup when it seems like there's no more people available.

He looks longingly into the distance. I think he's learned an accidental lesson today—fun things can happen on a walk. Well, besides sniffing and creating his masterpeeses.

As we turn, there's another surprise.

Prudence is walking toward us, and behind her, the rest of Bruce's household staff.

"We heard you're training him to be friendlier," Prudence says shyly. "Any chance we can also participate?"

"Of course." I toss her a quarter of a cookie. "Give him that and see what happens."

The bribe—I mean, treat—works like a charm, and Colossus quickly accepts Prudence as a friend, with Bob and Johnny after that.

"Mr. Roxford will be very pleased," Johnny says after he makes friends with the dog.

"Why?" I ask.

"No one at the local branches has a mustache," Johnny says as he twirls his pride and joy. "He said that it was my responsibility to represent the whole community."

Yeah. Now, if Colossus were to meet a dictator with a mustache—which most of them have—he would be cool as a cucumber. He'd also be fine with being stroked by a mustachioed villain on the set of a Bond movie called *The Chihuahua Who Loved Me*.

Grinning, I thank Johnny and lure Colossus back into the garage with my last piece of cookie.

As I take off my goofy helmet, I vow to never show my face at the local branch of Bruce's bank—though there isn't much I can do to make Prudence and the rest forget about my shame.

As usual, Colossus runs to locate Bruce once we enter the mansion, but when he notices that I'm walking to the kitchen, he pivots and goes with me.

"How are you not full?" I ask him. "At this point, with all those treats, you're probably skipping lunch."

Colossus brings his pointy ears together on the top of his head.

Full? I think that sensation is a myth, like Chupacabras, the Loch Ness Monster, or edible sugar-free cookies.

I check the fridge for something with fewer calories that I can use for further training and stumble upon the freshest-looking cucumbers I've ever seen.

Hmm. Bruce mentioned that Colossus eats cucumbers, and if that's true, the dog will get some much-needed post-walk hydration, along with a treat.

Roach wouldn't have eaten cucumbers so I'm a little skeptical about Bruce's assertion.

Cutting a small piece, I hand it to the dog.

Wow. He nearly bites off my finger in excitement as he snatches the cucumber. Making audible noises signaling deep satisfaction, Colossus devours the cucumber like a cannibal who got a hold of Bruce's (presumably) delicious liver.

"You like that, huh?" I ask Colossus.

Without my prompting, he plops his butt on the floor and looks me right in the eyes—a perfect execution of 'sit.'

Do I not want to sniff the big pile that a bear makes when he poops in the woods?

I give him another piece of cucumber and say the word 'sit,' hoping he will associate what he naturally did with the command.

He devours the cucumber with the same enthusiasm.

I cut another piece and hold it in front of his nose, then slightly above it—which causes canines to naturally sit. At the same time, I also say the command.

Yes!

He sits. I praise him both verbally and with a gift of vegetable—or fruit, if you're a botanical stickler.

I repeat the whole exercise.

He sits again.

And again.

"Wow," I say on his fifth successful attempt. "You're a quick learner."

He looks pointedly at the counter—where the rest of the cucumber is—then at me.

Is the moon not made of cheese? Is the sun not a big cookie right out of the oven?

Grinning, I cut up the rest of the cucumber, and we rehearse 'sit' some more—using just the word this time.

"I think you got it," I say when I have the last tiny piece of the treat left.

"Got what?" Bruce asks, startling me.

How did a man that big sneak up on me so stealthily? Do they teach ninjitsu at billionaire school?

"He's learned 'sit,'" I explain.

Colossus—who stood up to greet Bruce—plops his furry butt back on the floor, then looks at my reaction dutifully.

I give him the last of the cucumber, then look up in time to see Bruce smiling—and it's as startling as always. "I had a feeling he was a smart dog."

He did? "We met some of your people," I say, shifting from foot to foot. "And he befriended them all."

Bruce crouches in front of the puppy. "You did? Good boy."

Colossus lifts his little chin and wags his tail for all he's worth. To my shock, Bruce starts stroking his charge under said chin.

The puppy seems to enjoy the pets even more than food—and I'm left wondering if I could've been wrong about Bruce's feelings toward Colossus.

As inconceivable as it might seem, there's a chance this seemingly heartless man secretly loves this dog.

CHAPTER 19
BRUCE

etween "sit" and the gushing feedback from my staff about how "friendly" Colossus was when they saw him today, my chest fills with pride. I also feel kind of dumb because this is my dog learning basic dog niceties, not my son graduating cum laude.

Realizing I'm still petting the dog in front of Lilly and that she might disapprove of that for some dog trainer reason, I rise to my feet.

Hmm. She is looking at me strangely, but I don't know if that's condemnation or something else.

"Would you like to take a break?" I ask.

She cocks her head, a mannerism she no doubt learned from one of her fluffy students. "From what?"

"From him." I point down.

Her eyebrows come alive and meet in the middle of her forehead. "Why?"

I suppress another wave of irritation. First, she's

been pretending like that out-of-this-world kiss never happened, and now she's questioning my attempt to be cordial.

"I'll be videogaming," I grit out. "Colossus likes to sit on my lap when I do that. Or at least he does when I read. I figured—"

"The proper verb for playing video games is gaming," she chimes in. "That's what us 'kids' are calling it nowadays."

I turn my back to her. "I'm going to go do that, and my dog is coming with me."

"He'll need to get walked soon."

She sounds disapproving of being given time off—and they call *me* a workaholic.

"I'll do it," I say and feel my cock stirring as I recall how she taught me the dog-walking technique.

She huffs in grudging agreement.

As I stride away, for a second, I wonder if Colossus might choose to stay with her instead of go with me. She's fed him a lot, and as it turns out, his affection is easily bought.

But no.

I hear that signature clickety-clack of tiny nails on hardwood floors.

Wait.

I look down.

Yep.

The sea of pads has been removed. I guess Mrs. Campbell trusts him now—or trusts Lilly to do her job. Either way, a deal is a deal, so I take out my phone and make sure Lilly gets that bonus I mentioned to her.

When I enter the media room, I don't even get a chance to pick up the console before a videocall from my mother appears on my phone.

Setting Colossus on my lap, I accept the call. "Hi, Mom."

Mom's face looks eerily like Angela's—or is it more accurate to say it's the other way around? Biology obviously plays a small part in their likeness, but the larger and stranger resemblance came about after my sister convinced Mom to use her plastic surgeon. Or was *that* the other way around?

"Brucey, sweetie, how are you?" she asks, and though she hasn't smoked in forty years, she sounds like she never quit.

"I'm well. How about you?" I angle the phone to show Colossus on my lap, and predictably, instead of answering my question, my mother gushes about how cute "her grandson" is for what feels like an hour.

"My break will be over soon." I tap the watch on my wrist. "Was there any specific reason for your call?"

What I don't add is that usually, there *is*.

"Can't I call my son whenever I wish?"

I'm not sure if this one is biology or a plastic surgeon's doing, but the way Mom purses her lips is identical to the way my sister does it.

I sigh. "Obviously, you *can*."

"Good," she says. "Though it just so happens that I did want to talk to you about something."

Called it.

She smiles mischievously. "Or should I say... someone?"

Some people can't keep their fucking mouths shut. "What did Angela tell you?"

"That you got yourself a very *pretty* dog nanny," Mom says. "And that Angela disapproves of her already."

I scoff. "I'm not sure there's a woman in the world Angela would approve of."

Mom nods sagely. "I trust your judgment of character, so if you like this woman, I will too." I can hear the unsaid bit—*especially if that means grandchildren.*

"Lilly is just an employee," I say firmly.

"'Lilly,'" Mom says with an eyebrow waggle that I didn't think possible given all that Botox. "As in, *not* Ms. What-ever-her-last-name-is?"

This is how rumors start, so I'd better nip it in the bud. "She insists on being insultingly informal."

"And you go along with it?" Mom waggles her eyebrows again. "When is the wedding?"

"I've got to go," I say and reach for the hang-up button.

"Wait," Mom says. "Did I mention that we're coming over?"

My right eye twitches. "You're what?"

"Your father and I haven't seen you and Angela in ages," she says in a tone too accusatory, considering that "ages" is really two months in my case. "Since the two of you are going to be in the same place for once, we decided it was the perfect time to visit."

Since I'm rendered speechless, I simply nod as Mom tells me their itinerary—my acceptance a foregone conclusion.

"Are you excited?" she asks when she's done.

"I am," I say with a sigh. "But I'd better get back to work. There's a project I'm very passionate about that—"

"You're always passionate about your work," Mom says disapprovingly. "What is it this time?"

I explain to her how a cryptocurrency of my own making will help us bring banking to parts of the world where it is otherwise difficult—and she gives me her thoughts on this as a philanthropist herself.

"Thanks," I tell her when she's done. "But don't get me wrong. I intend to make money from this in the end."

"If your making money enriches people's lives, why not?" she asks.

I smile. "Exactly."

"I'd better let you go," she says. "But do make an effort to reply to my emails."

"Sure," I say. I'll have to delegate said task to someone besides my assistant because he is squeamish. Maybe *his* assistant? More than ninety percent of the videos my mom sends to people are grisly clips of someone getting their pimples popped. In fact, she is so obsessed with this disgusting activity that she went to medical school and became a dermatologist specializing in that one specific "treatment."

"Don't forget to spoil my grandson," she says with a grin. "See you soon."

With that, she hangs up.

I take Colossus outside using the leash techniques Lilly taught me—the ones that will be giving me wet dreams for years to come.

I'm not sure if it's the new skills, or the dog's training so far, but the walk goes smoother than in the past.

When I get back, I set the puppy on the floor and meet his gaze. "Ready to go back to Lilly?"

He becomes excited, which strongly suggests that what he heard was, "Want a snack?"

I let him follow as I seek Lilly out, but she's nowhere to be found.

"You're a dog," I say when I'm close to giving up. "Find Lilly."

Tail wagging, Colossus runs forward. I follow, but I'm pretty sure he'll lead me to his favorite place—the kitchen.

But no. We pass the kitchen, the media room, and the library before heading down a corridor into the gym—a place he's rarely, if ever, been.

Curious.

I enter the room.

Oh, fuck.

Lilly *is* here—and she is doing yoga. Specifically,

downward dog. Or to put it another way, she's bent over at the waist like she's ready for a hard fucking.

My breath hitches.

Her firm ass looks mind-bogglingly good in those tight yoga pants. Unbidden, a pornographic movie plays out in my mind's eye, one where I go into caveman mode and rip those yoga pants into shreds.

And there it is. A hard-on to rule them all. I've never taken Viagra, but I bet this is what an overdose of it would feel like.

As if taunting me, Lilly transitions into a yoga squat —or what she'd look like in reverse cow girl if she was bouncing on my cock.

Enough. I'm being a perv. It's best to back out of here before she notices me, so I can run straight into a cold shower.

I take a step backward, but it's too late. Tail wagging, the dog rushes over to Lilly's yoga mat. In an eyeblink, he's on his back in front of her, begging for a belly rub.

Lilly stands straight, then scans the nearby mirror until she spots my reflection. She then kneels (causing another cock twitch) and scratches Colossus's belly. "Where did you ditch Bruce?"

"I know you saw me," I growl.

"What's that?" She puts her ear next to Colossus's maw, like she's listening to him whisper something— and gets her ear licked for her trouble. "Ah, yes. He *can* be a real grouch."

"Very funny," I grit out.

Finally, she turns to me. "What are you doing here?"

I'm about to tell her that the dog led me here when I realize that may sound like a made-up excuse for being a peeping perv.

No. I should think of a better reason to be here.

And then it hits me.

I'm in the gym, so I might as well burn off some of this energy flowing through my veins. True, it might not be as effective as a cold shower, but it's better than nothing—and either way, I'm going to be late for my meeting.

Thus decided, I announce, "I'm here to box."

Lilly's eyebrows seem to dance a little jig—like two cute caterpillars that are on their way to turning into the most beautiful butterflies in the world. "Prudence mentioned that you box."

"She did?" I walk up to the nearby stand and grab my boxing gloves. "Does everyone here think nondisclosure agreements are just polite suggestions?"

Lilly winces. "I was obviously joking. She didn't tell me a thing. I read about your boxing online."

"Nice try." I take out my phone and tell Johnny to move the meeting I'm almost late to as is. The one good thing about running my own company is that, unlike everyone else, I don't *have* to show up to meetings unless I wish to. Of course, usually, I do wish to.

"Well," Lilly says. "You do your thing, and I'll try puppy yoga."

"Puppy yoga?" I ask. "Is that related to the puppy pose?"

"No," she says. "It's exactly as it sounds: doing yoga while there are puppies around. They get very curious and cuddly, and for obvious reasons, such yoga can be really soothing."

She gets into the cobra pose—chest out, back arched, arms in a push-up position, and lower body on the mat.

Predictably, Colossus thinks what she's doing is all about him, so he jumps on her lower back and sniffs her butt.

I can't help but smile. "Do puppy yoga classes incorporate the dogs into the poses?"

"They do, and so will I," she says, still staying in her position. "When I do the corpse pose, I'll encourage him to get on my chest, and during lotus pose, he can be on my lap."

Lucky dog. "I'm okay with this so long as Colossus is happy—and he's obviously having a blast."

"Great," she says. "I can do this daily if you'd like."

"Just tell me when," I say firmly—so I can avoid coming here at those times going forward, obviously.

"Will do," she says. "Now go do your boxing."

Ah. Right. Except I have a problem. I don't have my usual tank top on. Or shorts.

Then again, she doesn't know what I wear for this. I have boxers under these slacks that can pass for shorts, and lots of folks exercise shirtless.

There. Lilly goes into child's pose, which means she can't see me. Quickly undressing, I put on the gloves and get into my stance in front of the punching bag.

As I start the warm-up part of the workout, I realize that my ending up here in the gym was actually fortuitous. Between the kiss that I wish to forget and the family visit that is looming on the horizon, I've got a lot of pent-up energy—and this is a great way to burn it.

In the corner of my eye, I spot Lilly transitioning into the bridge pose.

Fuck. How can a move out of an ancient spiritual practice look so much like a scene from *Showgirls*?

I rip my gaze away from my dog's trainer and place it firmly on the punching bag. Inhaling sharply, I let the air out with a hissing sound and smash my fist into the bag.

CHAPTER 20
LILLY

Colossus runs away.

Hmm. Did he follow Bruce?

A hissing sound draws my attention—and when I turn, all the serenity that I've gained during the yoga practice is washed away by a tsunami of hormones.

Bruce is shirtless.

And pants-less.

With beads of sweat pebbling on his rippling muscles.

For Anubis's sake, even the dog is staring at Bruce as if saying:

He looks more masculine than a pack of boy dogs—and without so much as lifting a leg.

Bruce throws a devastating punch at the poor bag. And another.

Somehow, even the violence twisting his features is hot—so much so I feel unwanted heat pool in my core.

Grr. It's like this man is actively trying to keep me in a state of perpetual arousal.

Gritting my teeth, I start doing the cat-cow.

Nope. Unlike every other time I've done this, I become hyperaware of my pelvic floor muscles—so I switch to the lizard.

Hell's bells. This pose is even worse, and the happy baby leaves me feeling extremely unhappy. And wanting his baby.

The problem persists when I do the plow, and even when I do a shoulder stand, so I get back on my feet and attempt the eagle—standing on one foot, crossing my arms in front of my body, and hooking my right foot around my left calf.

Oh, no.

With my legs twisted like this, I've just put pressure on my oversensitive clit. If I keep the pose for even a second more, I might—

And it happens. I come in the middle of Bruce's gym—right in front of him. Holy shit. I've always had a hair trigger when it comes to orgasms, but this is a whole other level.

I untangle my legs and thank goodness no moans have escaped my lips—a feat that took an elephantine effort of will.

"Hey, Colossus," I say, my voice hoarse. "Let's go learn fetch."

Bruce pauses his onslaught to say, "His toys are by his bed."

Great. I'm headed to Bruce's bedroom.

At least he's not going to be there.

I exit the gym, but the dog doesn't follow.

With a sigh, I pick him up. I didn't think to bring a treat here and thus have nothing to lure him with.

When we're in Bruce's bedroom, I take a few toys and resist the strong urge to strip naked, dive into Bruce's bed, and reach another climax as I luxuriate in his smell on the sheets.

Noticing the toys, Colossus wags his tail.

Good. Now that I've got his attention, I take him to my room and toss the first toy—a plush shark that has some motor inside that makes it wag its tail.

The puppy runs after the shark, grabs it, but doesn't bring it back.

All right. I'm not going to use food for this. He's eaten too much today already, plus toys are all about fun, so if he doesn't want to play, I won't force the issue. What I do instead is pretend that I'm fascinated by his other toy—a small monkey that squeaks.

The gambit works. As soon as he notices how much fun I'm having with the monkey, he walks over to check it out—the shark still in his teeth.

As soon as he's within reach, I gush praise on him so he knows that walking over pleases me, and then I toss the monkey. Letting go of the shark, he runs after the new toy.

I repeat the whole thing a few more times and then wait to see what he does.

He brings the monkey to me, tail wagging.

"Good boy," I say as I reach for the toy. "Thank you."

Not so fast. He doesn't let go of the toy—which is a common dog behavior. Instead of fetch, he wants to play tug, and why not?

I play tug with him, letting him win a few times. When it's my turn to win, I toss the toy.

He brings it back.

We're halfway there already.

We keep playing like that for a while longer, and I watch him for any signs of needing to go potty—a common occurrence after playing. Nope. He simply walks over to my pile of dirty clothes and passes out.

I grin. This used to happen when Roach was a puppy too.

Using the little free time this gives me, I strip off my yoga clothes, rush to the bathroom to freshen up, and dress more presentably—in case I run into anyone during lunch.

No one specific... just anyone.

Once I'm dressed, I start reading *The Witcher* as I wait for the puppy to wake. Two pages later, my phone rings.

I pick up quickly. "Hello," I whisper.

"Hello to you too," Aphrodite says sardonically. "I demand a full status report."

In order to not wake Colossus, I take the call to the bathroom, where I grudgingly tell my cousin about the kiss.

The squeal on the other end of the phone is so high and loud I half expect the dog to wake up even though he's in a different room. "I told you so," Aphrodite says when she catches her breath. "Now remember, ovulation can last from twelve to forty-eight hours, so you're still in that window—and will be until tomorrow."

"He's pretending the kiss didn't happen," I say with an eyeroll. "Not that I'd let him anywhere near my eggs in any case."

"Sure, sure, sure. Nothing will happen—just like that kiss didn't."

I squeeze the phone tighter. "That's different."

"Yeah, yeah, yeah." I can somehow hear that she's got a stupid grin on her face. "Just use a condom when it 'doesn't happen.' Or not—all depending on the plans you do *not* have."

"Is there a term that's similar to fratricide, but for when you kill your cousin?" I ask.

"Hey, I'm on your side here," she says. "Newsflash: we're talking about a hot billionaire who also seems to be a good kisser."

"When did I tell you that he's a great kisser?"

"Never," she says. "But what you just said proves it."

My phone rings with a video call from my mom.

"I've got to go," I say. "Mom is calling."

"Oh, yeah," Aphrodite says sheepishly. "That's why I was calling. There is a tiny chance I might've told *my* mom about your new job… and you know how our moms are."

"Bye," I snap angrily and pick up Mom's call.

She and Dad are both on the other end, making this look suspiciously like a family meeting.

"I was just about to tell you," I say in lieu of a hello.

"About your *live-in* job?" Mom asks pointedly.

"Right, that. Everything happened so fast that—"

"You had time to tell Aphrodite," Mom says. "And she told the biggest gossip of the family."

Now isn't really the time to question who should have that particular title, but here's a hint: she's the person most upset she wasn't the first to know something juicy.

"Tell us about the man who hired you," Dad demands.

Mom turns to him. "That's sexist. No one said the rich employer was a man."

Dad sighs. "Tell us about *the person* who hired you."

Okay. I guess this will be like ripping off a Band-Aid. "Bruce Roxford."

I wince, expecting condemnation, but the expressions on both of their faces are blank.

"He owns that evil bank," I say.

They look even blanker.

I tell them the actual name of the bank in question. "You know," I add. "The place where you had your mortgage."

"Ah," Mom says.

"That's good," Dad says.

Huh? That's good? "Shouldn't you be a lot more upset? His bank took your house."

Mom shrugs. "That was unfortunate, but it wasn't personal."

It was for me.

"Besides," Dad says. "They were actually pretty nice to us, before the eviction at least."

"An oxymoron," I say with an eyeroll.

"Young lady," Mom says sternly. "Don't call your father names."

"Dad isn't the oxymoron. The phrase 'nice to us before the eviction' is."

"But they *were* nice," Mom says. "First, they gave us a deferment, then a forbearance."

I gape at them. "Why is this the first time I'm hearing any of this?"

Mom and Dad exchange glances. Eventually, she says, "Anytime the darn mortgage was mentioned back then, you'd try to give us all your money."

"And go on rants about how unfair life is," Dad adds.

I could've sworn my rants were about their bank, not life in general, but if that's how they remember it, who am I to argue?

"So... you're totally fine with me working for Bruce Roxford?"

Mom winks at me. "Sure. Working."

"Yes. Training his dog. What did Aphrodite say?"

Mom glances at Dad. "Not in mixed company."

Gah! If she doesn't want Dad to hear, there had to be a mention of ovulation, along with how hot Bruce is.

Colossus pitter-patters into the bathroom and stretches in front of me, like a cat.

"There he is," I say gratefully, angling the camera down. "My charge."

"So cute!" Mom squeals.

"Too small," Dad grumbles, but I know if he were here, he'd cuddle Colossus just as much as he did Roach back in the day.

Colossus starts to sniff around in a suspicious manner that I instantly recognize. "Mom, Dad, I have to run," I say. "He's looking for a bathroom."

"You're in a bathroom," Mom says.

"Yeah, that won't help him." I grab the little guy before he can have an accident. Dogs don't normally go when they're in your arms, though it would suck to be proven wrong this time. "Bye."

They wave goodbye, and we all hang up.

Once Colossus and I are outside, he starts making his masterpeeses all the way down the gorgeous path. Then, like déjà vu, the same exact attractive woman in high heels walks toward us. I think her name is Gertrude.

There's a key difference in this encounter, however. Gertrude has a leash in her hand with a tiny Yorkshire terrier on the other end of it.

"You have a dog?" I ask her from a distance.

She nods. "Mr. Roxford's assistant has rented dogs for everyone so that Colossus can socialize with them."

Wow. Talk about throwing money at problems. Where do you even "rent" dogs? Probably from someone rich, as this Yorkie looks like a specimen with a pedigree.

Time to socialize. I check my pockets and realize I don't have any treats.

Oh, well. It's not like the little Yorkie would hand them to Colossus anyway.

Turns out, Colossus *loves* Yorkies, or at least this one, because he's wagging his tail and sniffing her almost instantly. He even tries to play chase.

"Very cute," Gertrude says.

I have to agree, and this encounter is only the beginning. The next person from the local branch has a mini poodle—and Colossus loves him as much as the Yorkie. Same goes for the shih tzu that follows, and the pug after that.

"Maybe you didn't need me for this after all," I tell Colossus after another successful socialization encounter with a very calm German shepherd, a.k.a. dog number twenty. "You're very friendly with dogs."

Colossus looks up at me, the panting from all the excitement twisting his lips in that signature Chihuahua grin.

If human butts smelled as good as dog ones, I would've liked humans from the get-go as well. Now give me a cookie, please! It's been a hundred years since the last one.

"You know, I'm feeling a little peckish myself," I say and check the time.

Sure enough, it's almost lunchtime.

Now in sync in terms of our basic needs, we make a sharp U-turn and return to the mansion. Once Colossus is unleashed, he runs somewhere—probably to the kitchen.

I head over there and find Bruce eating.

He looks at me coolly. "Hello."

I look around. "Is the dog here?"

"He's supposed to be with you." And just like that, the coolness in his gaze turns into an arctic chill.

I open my mouth to explain that he ran ahead, perhaps to get one of his toys from my room, but the puppy shows up at that very moment.

Fuck me.

Based on what he has in his mouth, I was half right. He did run to my room to get something. It just wasn't his toy.

It was my panties.

CHAPTER 21
BRUCE

I gape at the lacy piece of fabric in my dog's mouth.

Could that be…?

Yep. Based on the blush spreading over Lilly's face, that's her underwear.

I repeat, lucky dog.

She dashes to get her undies, but Colossus decides he wants to keep them and escapes her grabbing hands.

"Please," she says. "Give that back."

He wags his tail but doesn't let go of the panties.

She's clearly distressed because the solution is pretty obvious here, and I'm not even a dog trainer.

Leaping to my feet, I walk up to the fridge and open it.

Just like that, Colossus releases the panties and rushes over to check what I'm about to pull out.

With a satisfied smirk, I get his food and set it on the floor.

As usual, he attacks it like his survival depends on this meal.

Lilly leaps for her underwear, but I catch a better look at it before she stashes it in her pocket.

It's a thong.

Fuck. That must be why her ass looked so good in those yoga pants.

And... I'm hard again. I sit back down at the table to hide it.

"That was a good idea," she mutters as she gets her lunch and sets it near me. "Thank you."

I was just about to chastise her about the choking hazard she created for my dog, but something about her rosy cheeks makes me swallow the criticism—along with a forkful of sweet potato mash.

"You still okay if I eat here?" she asks.

I nod, my mouth full.

"How are you liking the game?" she asks.

"Addictive," I reply, "but not as good as the source material. Speaking of, what do you think of the book?"

"I'll admit, it's great. But I'm not sure I want to even compare it to the game."

"Right," I say. "Because it would win."

She rolls her eyes. "Because it's like comparing apples and oranges."

"I don't get that idiom," I say. "Apples are better, obviously."

"That's the New Yorker in you talking," she says. "As a native Floridian, I'm contractually obligated to prefer oranges."

149

The conversation devolves into another New York versus Florida fight, but this one is less heated than before.

We're interrupted by Mrs. Campbell, who walks into the room carrying a stack of green squares.

"Ah, the lick mats," Lilly says. "Colossus will finally be able to savor a meal."

Curious, I let Lilly spread a little bit of peanut butter on one of the mats and hand it to the puppy as a test.

Interesting. It takes him a couple of minutes to do what usually would take a single heartbeat, and he seems to enjoy it rather than be frustrated, which I had feared.

Once again, Lilly was right.

I might just trust her from now on—when it comes to dog matters, that is. Either way, it's a rarity for me.

"Can I ask you something private?" Lilly asks, blushing again.

"You can ask," I surprise myself by saying. "I don't have to answer."

She waves her fork dismissively. "Forget it."

"I don't think I will be able to at this point," I say. "Just go ahead and ask me." And since when does she pretend to have tact?

She looks to the ceiling as if for divine help. "I already regret bringing it up."

"Bringing *what* up?" And why does my blood pressure always spike when she's around me?

"Fine." She bites her lip. "Does misophonia make it hard for you to date?"

I frown. Maybe it was a mistake to insist. Still, for some reason, I feel compelled to say, "People can date without having to eat together. There are museums. Opera. Golf." Am I overdoing it on activities people consider rich people clichés?

"You're right," she says. "I'm sorry."

I blow out a breath. "No. I know what you mean. I imagine it would be a problem in a serious relationship, especially after moving in together or something like that. None of mine have been serious so far, and I've been able to meet women who are willing to put up with a few eccentricities—especially when they get gifts that involve diamonds."

She rolls her eyes at that last bit—as I expected she might. There's definitely a socialist streak in her, or whatever you call people who don't like the wealthy.

"So…" she says cautiously. "Your current girlfriend has never seen you eat?"

I put my fork down. "My *current* girlfriend?" What sort of imaginary creature is that?

"Colossus's original mom," she says sheepishly. "You know… the woman from the video call."

"Angela?"

She nods.

I chuckle. "She's my sister—and it's *The Witcher* that I'm a fan of, not *Game of Thrones.*"

Lilly's cheeks flush once more, and I fight the odd

urge to peck one. "Now that you say it, that makes so much more sense. Why else would you adopt her dog?"

"Don't get me started on that last one. She's my sister, yet I'm still not sure why I said yes."

She glances down. "I think I do."

If she means the puppy is too cute to resist, she might have a point—not that I'm ready to admit that out loud. Especially not when the little troublemaker is listening. That way lie the most spoiled of dogs.

"What about you?" I ask.

She bats her thick eyelashes. "What about me?"

Nice try. "Does being a socialist interfere with *your* dating life?"

She snorts. "There's not much of a dating life to speak of."

Why do I like the sound of that?

"Nothing serious?" I clarify. "Ever?"

Wait. I should take that back. At work, the head of HR would tell me such questions are inappropriate.

What's worse is she's frowning—a rarity for her.

"I've only had one serious boyfriend," she says before I can backpedal. "But things ended badly."

My food suddenly loses all flavor. "What did he do?" And—completely unrelatedly—how much do assassins charge these days?

My tone must be rougher than I intend because she draws back. "He didn't hurt me or anything like that— if that's what you think. He had a short fuse, so we fought in front my dog a lot—who reacted just like Colossus did when you and I argued the other day."

Feeling a bite of guilt at the memory, I toss the dog a slice of cucumber from my salad—which he gladly devours.

"But then," she continues, "when Roach got sick—"

"Hold on," I say. "You dated someone named Roach?"

It would be too neat of a coincidence, considering the guy sounds like someone I'd want to squash.

"No. That's my late dog's name," she says. "My ex's name was Ennis."

That doesn't sound all that much better—as it's one 'p' added and one 'n' removed from "penis," which is what this guy sounds like. Or more accurately, a dick.

Then it hits me. "Roach is a reference to the Witcher's horse, right?" She really *is* as much of a fan of the game as I am of the books.

She nods. "So, as I started to say, when Roach needed surgery, Ennis thought it was a waste of money. We had a huge fight, and I finally ended things with him."

My hand clenches over my fork. "What kind of a man puts money ahead of a dog's life?"

"Spoken like a rich guy," she says.

"Touché. So what happened?"

"I decided it was worth spending the money on the surgery, and thanks to that, Roach went on to live another two wonderful years. Best money I've ever spent."

"I'm going to talk to my mother," I say firmly. "She might be interested in opening a fund that provides money for people who need it for medical care of a loved one, be they four-legged or human."

Her eyes light up. "Great idea. I've actually read about your parents' philanthropy. I think it's one of the more admirable things that the wealthy do."

Did Karl Marx think so too? I wonder what she'd think about my own philanthropic project—the one I've only recently felt ready to tackle.

She'll probably think I'm bragging, so it's best not to go into it.

"It's not my parents, plural," I say instead. "It's my mother who drives the philanthropy. Speaking of my parents—they're coming here. Angela too. With her *actual* boyfriend. Who isn't me."

"Har har. But wow. That's so exciting."

"Spoken like someone from a normal family."

She nearly chokes on her mashed potatoes. "You think *my* family is normal? On our last beach trip, my mom shaved my dad's chest hair into the shape of a bra. As in, he walked around looking like he was wearing a bikini made out bear fur."

I can't help the smile that tugs at my lips. "A few years back, my dad's best friend had a hangover and requested a Tylenol. As a prank, my dad gave him this special four-hundred-dollar pill instead, one that makes excrement look like it's made of gold." Her eyes widen, so I go on. "And if that's not enough, my mother built an ER in my parents' home."

"Wait," Lilly says, sounding faux shocked. "You *don't* have an ER on this estate?"

Now I'm full-on grinning. "You're right. That's a horrible oversight on my part. If I were to have a heart attack, I'd have to go to the same hospital as the hoi polloi."

She arches one of her mighty eyebrows. "Hoi polloi?"

"It means the masses." Or the proletariat, as her comrades would call it.

She shudders theatrically. "Oh, no. You mean the filthy wretches that dwell in the ninety-nine point nine-nine-nine percent? You wouldn't want to mix with the likes of *them*."

"This might be a good segue for something that we're doing this afternoon," I say. Initially, I was going to send her to do this by herself, but now I'm in the mood to join for some reason.

"Are we mainlining caviar?" she asks. "Or turning poop into diamonds?"

I shake my head. "We're going to the zoo."

"Oh. But what about all the hoi polloi there?"

"Not going to be a problem today," I say. "I booked the whole place."

She gapes at me. "Why?"

I gesture at the dog—who is, as always, sitting under foot and silently willing one of us to drop a morsel from our plates. "You said he needs to socialize with animals."

"Animals that he could meet in real life, like a cat or a squirrel. Not lions."

I shrug. "I figure if he's okay with a lion, he'll be

calm if he meets a cat. And if he's cool with seeing a capybara, no other rodent will frighten him, be it a squirrel or a New York rat."

She slowly shakes her head. "Fine, but why book the whole place?"

I narrow my eyes. "How can we control the situation if the regular patrons are there?"

"I guess that makes some warped kind of sense... in a universe where you're *trying* to spend as much money as possible."

"Should we not go?" Even asking the question makes me feel disappointed for some reason.

"Can you get a refund?" she asks.

"Of course not. The place is already empty."

"In that case." She looks down at Colossus with a toothy grin. "We're headed to the zoo."

CHAPTER 22
LILLY

As I dress and apply makeup for the zoo trip, I catch myself feeling overly excited—like I'm prepping for a date.

What the hell? Is it because I learned that Bruce is single? Or because he shared his dating woes with me —assuming you could even consider what he told me "woes?"

I curb my enthusiasm somewhat, but I still end up looking my best—and why not? Maybe there will be a cute zookeeper at the gorilla exhibit.

By the time I get to the kitchen, the chef is explaining the dinners he's packed for all of us, including Colossus. He's even chopped up a cucumber for treats and baked tiny cookies.

Colossus looks longingly at the cooler where his treats are stashed.

"Didn't you *just* have breakfast?" Bruce asks him.

Colossus tears his eyes away from the cooler and

stares up at his human with a gaze that would melt the hearts of Cruella de Vil, The Wicked Witch of the West, and Martha Stewart combined.

I want a snack now. It's been ages since breakfast. Ages, I tell you. How can I be expected to function on such an empty stomach?

Bruce shakes his head ruefully, walks over to the cooler, and pulls out one of the cucumber bits.

Okay. He's not bothering to keep it a secret anymore—he's crazy about the puppy—and that's as sexy as the boxing.

He would probably deny it if I accused him of being in love with the dog, but I know the signs. I'm starting to show some of them myself.

"The limo is ready," Johnny informs us and picks up the cooler.

When we get inside the limo, I point at a bag-like contraption attached to a seat and ask Bruce what it is —though I have a theory.

"A car seat for the dog," Bruce says, which is what I figured. "Custom made and crash tested."

There you go. Another sign that he adores this dog.

Also, did he crash another limo to test the doggy car seat? I wouldn't be surprised. If there are multiple ways to do something, Bruce will go for the one that costs the most.

After strapping Colossus into the contraption— there are harness-like straps and everything—Bruce descends into the adjacent seat, tells me to "buckle up," and does the same himself.

I presume he wants me to sit as close to my charge as possible—which just so happens to be right next to Bruce as well. So I take that seat, fully ready to be told to move a few seats away if Bruce demands it because it's almost comical for us to be so close in an otherwise empty limo.

Nope. Bruce either doesn't care or is okay with my proximity.

Then again, I'm not sure I'm okay with it myself. I'm still getting intermittent flashbacks to him boxing, plus we're close enough for me to feel the heat radiating from his powerful body and to detect the yummy scent of cucumber on his fingers, which makes me want to lick—

"How badly am I interrupting your curriculum with this trip?" Bruce asks, bringing me out of my hormone-inspired reverie.

I shrug. "It's not like I'm helping Colossus cram for his finals."

Colossus must know we're talking about him because he wags his tail.

I'll take the finals if a cookie is on the line. And cucumber. And belly scratches. But mostly the cookie.

The limo pulls out, and we ride in silence for a minute or two. I get the feeling it feels companionable to Bruce, even if it seems awkward to me.

"What do you do for fun?" I blurt and then instantly cringe. Despite our date-like destination, this isn't a date—but the question *is* date-like.

To my relief, he doesn't chastise me for prying.

Instead, he furrows his forehead, acting as if "fun" is something you have to contemplate as hard as the meaning of life, the universe, and the number forty-two.

"Define 'fun,'" he finally says.

I chuckle with an accidental snort. "Fun is something you do to enjoy yourself."

"Well... I enjoy my work."

"No," I say. "I enjoy training dogs, but I can't say 'work' if someone asks me what I do for fun. I'd say video games. Or going bowling with my cousin. Or going to the beach to watch the sunset. That sort of thing."

He rolls his eyes. "Fine. Reading."

I match his eyeroll. "You don't say. Let me guess—you like *The Witcher* books. I must be psychic.'"

"I enjoy cooking," he says grudgingly.

"Now that's more like it," I say but privately wonder why anyone with a private chef would want to cook. Though maybe I wonder that because I can't cook to save my life and don't enjoy it. "Anything else?"

He shakes his head. "I don't have time for anything else. There are one hundred and twelve waking hours in a week, and I work eighty of them. Of the remaining thirty-two, I spend seven on exercise and about twenty-one on eating and other bodily functions. That leaves only four hours of free time, which is about half an hour per day. Most hobbies require a greater time commitment, but reading is perfect, as is cooking when you don't have to."

I'm not sure if I should mock or pity a billionaire who has so little fun in his life. "What about taking walks on your giant estate?" I ask. "Fishing in the lakes you own, or kayaking? How about watching movies in your personal movie theater? Or swimming—be it in that giant pool you own or your private beach? Or how about—"

"No time," he says. "But I might do all of those things. One day."

I exhale an exasperated breath. "It's like all your money is wasted on you."

His jaw muscles tick. "If I *were* interested in having fun, I wouldn't have all this money." He gestures around the fancy limo.

I wave his point off as if it were an irksome fly. "If you don't stop to have fun, what's the point of making all this money? And besides, your parents are rich, so you would have money even if you didn't work like a maniac."

He scoffs. "I think you misunderstand the difference between billionaires like me and millionaires like my parents."

I can't believe he said that with a straight face. "I'm sure said difference is not as vast as the difference between millionaires and people like me."

"Wrong," he says. "If you make a middle-class salary, you can make a million in twenty or so years. To make a billion, it would take twenty-two thousand years."

"I think we've found your hobby," I say. "Useless

math and hoarding more money than you could possibly spend."

He smirks. "The proletariat has spoken again."

"So has the bourgeoisie," I retort with a huff.

The limo stops, and I sneak a peek out the window.

That's not the zoo. Given where we are, we haven't actually left the enormous estate yet.

"That's the helipad," Bruce explains.

I unbuckle my seatbelt. "The helicopter *is* a dead giveaway."

"Sorry it took so long to get here," Bruce says. "I should have built the helipad closer to the house."

"Yeah, I hate it when I have to drive to my helicopter too. What does a chopper have to do with the zoo?

He smirks. "It will get us there."

I unbuckle Colossus's seat. "You realize we just drove almost half the distance it would've taken to get to the zoo." As in, he's taking the whole "do it the most expensive way" much too far.

Bruce unbuckles his seatbelt. "We're not going to the Palm Beach Zoo."

"Oh?"

"I prefer the one in Miami." He holds the door for me as the driver grabs the cooler.

"Miami?" I whisper to Colossus. "I was half expecting him to say we're headed to Zoológico de Chihuahua—in Mexico."

Exiting the car, we head over to the helicopter where a pilot is already waiting.

"Has Colossus ever flown?" I ask Bruce as we take our seats.

"A few times," Bruce says. "I think he likes it."

Huh. Should I admit that I'm a helicopter virgin?

Nah.

I just strap in and swallow my overexcited heart back into my throat.

The motors roar, and we lift off.

The noise is so deafening that speaking isn't possible—not that I mind since all I want to do is gawk at the glorious scenery below.

To my shock, Bruce takes out the Nintendo Switch and starts playing *The Witcher 3*.

Spoiled much? Even if I'd ridden this helicopter a thousand times, I'd still want to be looking out the window—and I'm that video game's biggest fan.

All too soon, the helicopter lands right in an empty parking lot that's not at all a helipad. No doubt only the likes of Bruce get permission to do something like that.

Unstrapping, we leave our fancy ride behind and head over to the zoo entrance.

I walk Colossus on a leash, and he must smell the nearby animals already—because he wags his tail excitedly.

Before we can enter the zoo proper, a disheveled, austere-looking older gentleman crosses our path, his expression of disapproval almost palpable.

"Mr. Roxford?" he half-asks, half-states.

"Yes." Bruce extends his hand. "And you are?"

"I'm *Doctor* Smith." He grasps the proffered hand

like he wants to keep it. "According to the president, you need someone with a PhD in zoology for your little date?"

Little date? Is that supposed to be me? Also, I hope the "president" is the one in charge of this zoo, not this country.

Bruce rips his hand out of the weird handshake. "Excuse me?"

Dr. Smith wrinkles his button-like nose. "I was trying to say that I have more important things to do than be a glorified tour guide."

I've never seen a worse case of giving attitude to the wrong person. Bruce's expression turns practically arctic, and I half expect water droplets to condensate on his skin, like on a soda can fresh from the fridge.

"There's been a misunderstanding," Bruce says, each word dripping with liquid nitrogen. "We don't need any help from a pompous fuckwit."

Like he's trying to punctuate the words, Colossus growls at Dr. Smith—no doubt picking up on Bruce's attitude.

"Are you taking that furry rat into the zoo with you?" Dr. Smith asks, sounding appalled.

Colossus looks at Bruce, then at me—clearly unsure if he should escalate the growl to a bark at this juncture.

I'm not a rat. I'd never betray my comrades, even for a cucumber... Maybe not even for a cookie.

"Look, mister," I say, figuring it's best to prevent Bruce from knocking this idiot out and then having to pay a seven-figure settlement later. "You said you're too busy—great! Why don't you go do whatever it is you need to do." Fucking oneself would be preferable, but I'm not a stickler.

"Right. Just don't enter any of the habitats," Dr. Smith says snidely. "And don't let that thing out of your sight, or something will eat it." He points at Colossus.

"Super helpful," I say with an eyeroll. "Now, how about you go shovel gorilla shit—or whatever it is you do here?"

Bruce's expression warms instantly. He pulls out one of the micro-cookies the chef prepared and gives it to Colossus. Just like that, Colossus forgives everything —and forgets.

With a huff, Dr. Smith turns on his heel and strides away, unsurprisingly walking like he's got a broom up his ass.

"After you," Bruce says, gesturing for me and Colossus to enter first.

We do, and despite a slightly annoying start, I feel myself getting excited.

The excitement grows stronger when Bruce reveals that he has rented a two-person golf-cart-like cycle so that we can pedal around the zoo grounds instead of walking.

"Why?" I ask.

"You know how much Colossus likes to mark his territory?" he asks.

I nod.

"We won't get far if we traverse the zoo on foot, but this should help. Do you mind?"

"Of course not," I reply, and it's almost true. If I did mind, it would be because of how date-like this mode of transportation feels. Or maybe *romantic* would be a better word?

"Great." Bruce secures Colossus in the cycle's compartment that is usually meant for children. "Do you want to be the one driving?"

I graciously take the side of the cycle that has a fake steering wheel. "Since you're paying, you might as well get to drive."

Then again, he is usually chauffeured everywhere, so perhaps—

Nope.

I can tell he's excited to be the one driving. How else to explain the enthusiastic way he begins to pedal, moving the two-seater without my help?

I start to help him after a minute, but we stop very soon, next to an exhibit that appears empty at first— with just a moat surrounding an island with an Indonesian temple in the center.

Colossus's little nose becomes hyperactive, so there's clearly an animal to be sniffed, if not seen.

And then, I spot one.

A tiger.

CHAPTER 23
BRUCE

At the sight of the giant cat, Lilly tenses, but Colossus just stares at the killing machine with a curiosity he usually reserves for stuffed toys, robotic vacuum cleaners, and new shoes.

Note to self: if I ever go on a safari, the dog will stay behind because he might just sniff the butt of a tiger if he got the chance.

Snapping out of her reverie, Lilly rewards Colossus's chill behavior with a treat. Then we move on, stopping only when we spot a crocodile nearby.

This time, Colossus seems a little perturbed by what he sees, which is probably for the best as Florida teems with that creature's alligator cousins, and few Chihuahuas would survive trying to befriend one of them. Then, as though trying to prove how bad he is at telling apart dangerous animals from benign, Colossus barks at the Malayan tapir.

"I know, sweetie," Lilly says soothingly. "That thing needs to decide if it's a pig or an ant eater."

Somehow, her words calm the puppy, and as soon as he's quiet, she reinforces the behavior with a cookie.

"Tapirs are actually related to horses and rhinoceroses," I can't help saying.

Lilly sticks her tiny little tongue at me. "And here I thought getting rid of Dr. Smith would mean we'd skip boring lectures."

Fuck. Could I forbid her from doing that again, and anything else involving that delectable tongue, especially while I'm trying to pedal? Bikes and hard-ons definitely don't mix.

Nah, bad idea. At best, I could politely request it. But with her being a contrarian, that would be like giving her a cookie. She'd just do it more.

Colossus begins barking again, this time at an orangutan.

"Hush," Lilly says to him soothingly. To me, she says with a grin, "Not that you can blame him. He probably thinks that's your chef, naked."

I burst out laughing. Now that Lilly has pointed it out, the resemblance is uncanny.

Hearing me laugh seems to calm the dog, and Lilly gives him a treat again before we move on to the exhibit with the sloth bear.

Of course. Colossus wags his tail at the bear.

"Is it possible he's smart enough to suck up to dangerous animals?" I ask Lilly. "And pester only the ones who can't eat him?"

"I'm pretty sure the chef—I mean, the orangutan—could be a danger to a dog Colossus's size."

We proceed, and Colossus proves my theory wrong when he's happy to see the meercats but barks at an elephant. Around the lion enclosure, he wags his tail, but he also does it for a camel.

"Maybe he decides his attitude based on smell?" I mutter. "Or on the shapes of the clouds above us?"

Lilly gestures into the distance. "This next stop should be interesting."

She's right. In the next habitat, we spot African painted dogs.

Huh. They must smell enough like a regular dog for Colossus to want to go sniff their butts, and he looks disappointed when he's not allowed to do so.

We ride over to the next habitat, one with hyenas.

Colossus begins to growl.

Lilly soothes him. "I know, sweetie. No one likes them—not since they helped Scar with his evil plans against Simba and Mufasa."

But didn't the hyenas redeem themselves somewhat when they dispatched Scar at the end?

Whatever his reason for disliking them, after the hyenas, Colossus seems to be in a bad mood and barks at gazelles, then antelopes, followed by oryx and addax.

"Maybe he doesn't like them because of all those horns," Lilly says with a wide grin. "Think about it: they're big and they're horny."

I chuckle and don't add that by her logic, Colossus should also bark at me since I'm pretty big, and being around Lilly keeps me hornier than a teen who's just discovered the internet.

As we proceed forward, there seems to be even less logic for Colossus's likes and dislikes. He's glad to see the pigmy hippo but not the black rhino, barks at gorillas but is happy to see chimpanzees—even though the latter seem to be playing hot potato with their feces. After that, he wags his tail when he spots the giraffes, but he growls at their close cousin, the okapi.

We keep going like that until we reach the giant Galapagos tortoises—who happen to be humping each other's brains out as we approach.

Blushing, Lilly clears her throat. "Well, then. This is awkward."

Yeah. They look like two tanks going at it in slow motion, and the dog seems fascinated by the spectacle, while I just feel jealous.

"They're taking a while," Lilly says after we stand there in fascination for at least a few minutes. "They must be practicing turtle tantra."

"They're the longest-lived land vertebrates," I say. "It would make sense if their coitus was also the longest lasting."

Colossus yawns—probably getting bored of the horny reptiles. I drive us over to the next attraction, which happens to be the harpy eagle.

Colossus's reaction is completely neutral, like the bird doesn't even exist.

"Do you think he's getting tired of seeing so many animals all at once?" I ask.

"Probably," Lilly says. "And it *is* getting close to his dinner time."

She's right. I pick up speed and drive us to a little spot by a stream where our picnic is already set up.

"Wow," Lilly says when she sees it. "That's pretty nice."

If by nice, she means unnecessarily romantic, then I'd have to agree. For me and Lilly, there's a cozy blanket on the grass with wine and a veritable buffet of hors d'oeuvres. For Colossus, there's a baby-gate-enclosed space covered by a net (to protect from birds of prey) and a variety of blended foods spread over lick mats to stimulate his tastebuds for at least a few minutes.

Taking a seat, I grab a smoked trout croquette and gesture for Lilly to join me. She does, and as she devours a date stuffed with goat cheese, I do my best not to stare too much at her mouth—no matter how fascinating it is.

"Was that okay?" she asks, looking self-conscious. "I promise I'll chew the next morsel a bit more."

I look at her with a confused expression, until it hits me. "You mean my misophonia?"

She nods.

"I completely forgot about that," I say, awed. "The first time that's ever happened."

CHAPTER 24
LILLY

His admission makes me feel more special than the Green Berets—and not for the first time.

Still, just in case, I take the smallest stuffed tomato and eat it with as little chewing as possible. Then, mostly to get his attention away from my eating, I ask, "When you said a billion is a much bigger amount of money than a million, I got to wondering... Why do you need so much money in the first place?"

He considers this over a crostini. "I know you think there's income inequality here in the U.S., and I won't argue that point, but if you look at the world as a whole, that's where a much bigger inequality comes into play—and I've been wanting to do something about that. Doing something, however, requires wealth in the billions rather than the millions."

I'm speechless. The guy I thought was the human equivalent of Scrooge McDuck actually cares about income inequality? "What exactly are you going to do?" I find myself asking.

He tells me. His explanation gets kind of technical, but as best as I can understand, he's soon going to release a cryptocurrency into the world, one that will allow people who don't have access to banks to pay electronically where they couldn't before. More importantly, the crypto will allow wealthy individuals to donate money to people directly—something Bruce is planning to pioneer.

"But isn't there cryptocurrency already?" I ask. "Bitcoin and the like?"

"Mine will be more ecofriendly," he says. "And hopefully more stable."

"Wow," I say. "This puts your workaholism in an almost angelic light."

"Well, then I should give you the full disclosure," he says. "I do expect that in the end, I'll end up getting even richer—assuming I don't decide to donate the new money I'll make off this initiative."

"How?"

He proceeds to explain it, but I only vaguely understand and am too embarrassed to admit it.

"How about you?" he asks when he's finished talking in crypto-jargon. "Do you have a big goal that you're trying to accomplish?"

I'm not sure if it's the nice day we've spent together, or the fact that I feel us vibing in a major way, or the memory of that kiss, but I put all my cards on the table—or rather, blanket. "I want to train service dogs."

Frowning, he halts the path of a tiny cucumber sandwich that was headed into his mouth. "I thought that's what you do *now*. Didn't you tell me about training your cousin's dog to sniff out infertility?"

"The dog smells when someone *is* fertile, and yes, I did do that, but that has been my only service dog so far. Sorry if I made it sound like I've trained more. Using the money from this job, I plan to attend a specialized school and get a bunch of certifications."

He nods approvingly. "Let me know if you need any money up front to pay for said school and the like. Also, now that Colossus is socialized, I can make it so that someone from the household staff watches him as you study for a few hours a day."

By Anubis, if he's going to experiment with being nice, and during such a romantic picnic no less, I can't be held responsible for my actions (or panties coming off).

"Oh, and if you *can* think of a service dog specialization for Colossus, I'd be very interested to hear it," he adds.

The idea comes to me in a flash. "What about your misophonia?"

Shit. My stupid reminder seems to evaporate his good mood. "How could a dog help with that?"

"You tell me," I say. "He could provide emotional support when you need it, or I could teach him to bark at anyone caught chewing in your vicinity. That way, you're not the only one bothered by an annoying sound."

He perks up. "You could teach him that?"

I nod. "Food already gets his attention, and we know he can bark from earlier, so combining the two shouldn't be that hard."

A mischievous gleam enters his eyes. "How quickly can you do it?"

I shrug. "When do you need it done by?"

"Tomorrow," he says.

"Why?"

He sighs. "My family doesn't really respect my condition. It might be nice if Colossus polices their behavior."

There's a lot of information packed in that statement, but I don't have time to psychoanalyze at the moment. I'm frantically trying to figure out the most efficient training regimen… and coming up short. Not unless… "What if we cheat?"

Bruce arches an eyebrow.

"I could teach him to bark when he spots a gesture command," I explain. "You could then stealthily do the gesture if someone eats around you—but we could *tell* them he's barking because he's a misophonia service dog."

My reward is one of those rare smiles that turn his face into the epitome of handsome. "How about this for a gesture?" He massages his temple with his right index finger.

"I think I could get him to bark in response to that very quickly. Possibly even this evening. I just need to know what currently makes him bark so I can mark the behavior."

"Rubbing alcohol," he says. "I applied some after I cut myself shaving one time. He was barking as if I were a gorilla."

"He must hate the smell," I say with a thumbs up.

"That's what I figured."

I reach for a miniature quesadilla, and he does the same—and our fingers brush.

Oh, wow. This must be how Frankenstein's monster felt right after that reanimating jolt of lightning.

Quesadilla forgotten, we lean toward each other, pulled by whatever energy our fingers just exchanged.

I moisten my lips. He watches me hungrily, then dips his head. Just as our lips touch, there's a canine whine.

We fly apart like two magnets with polarities reversed.

Flushing, I turn and see that—unsurprisingly—the pitiful sounds are coming from Colossus's enclosure. He must've finished his lick mats, saw us headed toward kissing, and felt left out.

"He probably wants to go home," Bruce says.

Yeah. Sure. The dog wants to go home, not his dad who once again regrets almost kissing "the help."

I touch my unsatisfied lips. "Great. That should give me more time for his training."

Bruce leaps to his feet and extends his hand to help me get up. Pretending I don't see the proffered appendage, I stand up on my own and get Colossus out of the enclosure and into his harness.

We don't talk much on the trip back to the helicopter, and the noise during the flight doesn't let us interact on the way back to the estate.

"Do you have any rubbing alcohol here?" I ask Bruce when we get into the limo. "I want to get a head start on the training." And if that means we won't have to talk—or feel tempted to kiss—all the better.

He rummages in the first-aid kit, but it turns out it has an antibiotic ointment instead of rubbing alcohol for disinfecting. Scooching over to the bar, he grabs a bottle of Absolut Crystal and asks Colossus, "Would you bark at vodka?"

Colossus wags his tail. No doubt the question he heard was, "Want a cookie?"

"Let's test it out." I prepare a cookie. "Open the bottle, dip a napkin in it, and let him get a whiff."

When he's almost done with the prep, I add, "Put your finger to your temple so he can see."

Bruce lets Colossus sniff the vodka. The puppy barks.

This smell is an affront to olfactory perception—and this is coming from someone who luxuriates in the aroma of a ripe butt.

Belatedly, Bruce touches his temple, and I give Colossus a cookie.

"Now try just the temple bit," I say.

Bruce does, but it's not working yet, so we involve the vodka again and a couple of more times after that.

By the end of the limo ride, Colossus begins to understand what we're trying to do and sometimes barks when Bruce touches his temple.

"We'll work on this more for the rest of today," I say when we come to a stop.

"Yes," Bruce says imperiously. "Do that."

———

"Ready to call it a night?" I ask Colossus when I catch myself yawning for the tenth time.

He cocks his head and gives me puppy eyes.

Sure, but can I request dreams in which I eat cookies?

"Don't look at me like that," I say when the sadness in said puppy eyes intensifies. "Fine. How about one more—but last one?" I put my finger to my temple.

The puppy barks triumphantly and proudly accepts his treat. He's now fully mastered this trick and is ready to learn to bark under different conditions.

I check the clock.

It's way past bedtime.

"Go to sleep." I point at the tiny replica of Bruce's bed that someone so helpfully brought over while we were at the zoo. "This is your new room."

Colossus walks over to sniff the bed, then grabs the bedding with his teeth and starts dragging it—unsuccessfully.

Maybe he wants it farther from the wall? I move the bed a little, but the dragging behavior doesn't stop.

Weird. Is it some ritual or an odd way to tuck

himself in? Perhaps he's working his way up to having his way with the bed? Roach would hump his bed upon occasion. And the pouf next to my recliner. And the broom.

Leaving Colossus to do whatever it is he's up to, I undress, grab my nightie, and head to the bathroom for a shower. As the warm water pelts my skin, I close my eyes, but that causes some unwanted images to enter my mind—ones involving Bruce, his lips, and other body parts.

That does it. Once I get into bed, I'm going to release some of this sexual tension with one of my toys.

Plan in place, I exit the shower, dry myself, and put on the nightie—then remember I haven't yet brushed or flossed my teeth. I'm mid-way through my brushing when I hear a heart-wrenching whine that sounds eerily like a baby's cry.

Swallowing toothpaste, I run barefoot to see what's wrong.

Looking miserable, Colossus sits next to his bed, whining.

"I'm here," I tell him soothingly. "Go to sleep."

He doesn't listen, and nothing I try works—from belly rubs to behind-the-ear scratches.

Time for the big guns. Picking him up, I take him to my bed. If this is a big no-no for Bruce, he can chastise me for it later.

The whining continues. I begin to suspect what Colossus wants—the clue is that his little nose points unerringly at the door.

"Do you want Daddy?" I ask.

He whines again.

"He's probably already sleeping," I say. "He'd be grumpy if we woke him." Or murderous.

Another whine.

"Seriously. Any chance you can wait till tomorrow?"

Nope. The puppy seems inconsolable.

Oh, well. My chances of getting fired have just skyrocketed. Sliding my bare feet into slippers, I take Colossus in one hand and his bed in the other and traverse the mansion—which seems to have grown just for this occasion.

When I reach Bruce's room, I'm panting and there's sweat beading on my temples. On the bright side, Colossus goes quiet, confirming my theory.

"Please behave," I beg the puppy. "My best bet is sneaking you in and getting out before Bruce wakes up."

Praying the door doesn't creak, I open it just a sliver.

Crap.

It's pitch black in comparison to the hallway.

I close my eyes and will them to adjust to the dark. At the same time, I pet Colossus and hope he doesn't whine so close to his goal.

My strategy pays off. When I open my eyes, I can see into the bedroom well enough to sneak in.

Channeling my inner ninja, I hold my breath and tiptoe to the doggie bed's former location.

Okay. I'm there and undetected thus far.

Setting the bed down, I put Colossus into it.

Yes! I did it, and Bruce is none the wiser—until tomorrow morning, that is.

I go into stealth mode once again and turn toward the door. That's when a fat bead of sweat on my right temple starts to feel unbearable, and I absentmindedly wipe it off.

Colossus barks.

Shit.

I'm an idiot. I've just spent hours training him to bark when he sees someone's temple being touched, and I just inadvertently gave him the command.

"Alexa, bedroom lights on!" Bruce shouts—and I feel a sense of déjà vu as I go blind for a moment.

Turning toward my doom, I squint against the brightness overhead—and my eyes threaten to leap out of my head and grow tongues so they can lick some of what they're seeing.

Wearing absolutely nothing, Bruce is almost upon me, his gaze at its icy best, his every muscle rippling, and Titan fully erect, jutting out like the chiding index finger of a giant.

Driven by pure adrenaline, I back up a step and then one more... which is when I step on the edge of Colossus's bed and lose my balance.

My hands begin to flail.

Oh, no. If I fall on the tiny dog, I'll hurt him. So, I do the only thing I can to save him—let myself pitch forward, right at Bruce.

CHAPTER 25
BRUCE

see Lilly flailing and can almost picture her tiny head hitting the floor—and the damage that would result.

No. Not on my watch. With adrenaline boosting the capabilities of my muscles to levels I didn't think possible, I leap forward and manage to catch her in my arms just in time.

Even like this, I can tell the air has been knocked out of her—but this is nothing compared to the nightmare that could've been. In fact, when I think about it, my mom's home ER doesn't sound so frivolous anymore.

I'm building one. First thing tomorrow.

Catching her breath, Lilly blinks up at me, her green-tinged hazel eyes frightened and her eyebrows so animated that if they started speaking in morse code and proved to be independently sentient, I wouldn't be surprised.

"You caught me," she gasps.

"Barely." And since I'm unsure whether she'll tumble again if I set her on her feet, I carry her toward my bed instead. When she's safely splayed on the mattress, I ask, "Are you okay?"

She nods.

"Are you on drugs?" I demand.

She blinks her eyelashes at me. "Drugs?"

I nod at Colossus—who's already sleeping soundly, like his trainer didn't just almost break her skull. "Bringing the dog here. Losing your balance. Drugs and alcohol are the more benign explanations that come to mind. As far as I know, you don't have vertigo, or—"

"I just tripped," she says, looking anywhere but at me. "You were there, naked, so I stumbled."

"Oh." I realize that I'm still naked, and that this isn't socially acceptable, especially since my cock is still—

"The dog was missing you," she says with gathering confidence. "He started whining, so I brought him here. If you're going to fire—"

"Thank you. I don't like it when he's sad." Now that I know she's isn't about to have an overdose and is otherwise safe, I take in her outfit, or lack thereof, and immediately regret doing so because it makes my erection become almost painful in its intensity.

She locks eyes with me. "You *do* care." As if to highlight her words, she wantonly scans my naked body as a blush spreads from her cheeks and deep into her nightie.

Why does she draw me in like that? It's like she's a cookie, and I'm my dog. Without meaning to, my lips form three words. "I do care."

And that's it. It's like a dam is broken. She arches toward me, and I close the remaining distance in a blink. Then my mouth is devouring hers, and it's as exquisite as before, only more raw and passionate.

But no. I pull away. "We can't."

Her lips part, all tempting and pink. "Why not?"

Where do I start? "You work for me."

She scoffs. "I couldn't care less."

"There's also—"

"I know you want to." She glances at my cock.

"Want? I need you, but—"

She shakes her head vehemently. "No buts."

Fuck it. I kiss her again, and not just her lips, but also her deliciously tiny neck, her dainty collarbone, her delicate shoulder… Breathing hard, I pull away to give her a chance to come to her senses—but she slithers out of her nightie instead.

"Wow," I mutter reverently. "You're gorgeous."

"So are you," she breathes, and then she does the sexiest thing I've ever seen in my life—second only to her yoga poses and that leash training she put me through.

Getting on all fours, she crawls up the bed, near where my pillows are, her perky little ass as close to perfection as things can be outside of the realm of pure mathematics.

Does she realize what she's doing? My heartbeat is

pounding in my temples and my nostrils flare like those of a wild beast.

Over her shoulder, she murmurs, "Do you have protection?"

Nearly ripping a drawer from its socket, I snatch a condom out of the nightstand. "Are you sure about this?" My words are a low growl.

"Positive." She slightly spreads her legs, giving me a glimpse of pink.

Fucking fuck. I'm going to explode. The next few seconds are blurry—probably because my cock is monopolizing all the blood, leaving little for my brain. Pulling her to me, I kiss my way down her body until I reach the pink pussy that I glimpsed, and then I lose myself in it, licking her folds like it's my last meal.

She moans, spurring me on, and I slide a finger inside her to feel the velvety warmth that I've been dreaming about ever since we met.

Oh, shit. She feels better than in my dreams. All I want to do is get inside her—but I resist. I must have her come like this.

Her moans become more desperate.

Yes! I'm about to lose it.

Time to bring it home. Gathering the rapidly unraveling shreds of my self-control, I rest my tongue on the little bud of her clit and press on the same region with my finger from the inside.

Her moans turn to screams, and then her body trembles as her pussy squeezes around my finger.

Her orgasm unlocks something primal inside of me.

Capturing her gaze, I pull out my finger and lick every drop of her from it.

"I want you inside," she breathes as she tears open the condom wrapper and envelops my cock.

With something like a growl, I pick her up and set her the way I want—on all fours, just like when she crawled for me.

She reaches over, grabs my cock and guides it to the promised land as I grab her buttocks, hard.

It takes all my willpower to thrust slowly. Once. Twice. Then, when I feel her yielding, I piston into her with everything I've got.

"Yes!" she screams.

I almost come right then and there. But I don't. Impossibly, I speed up, thrusting like our lives depend on me getting deeper and harder—like this is my reason for being.

She moan-screams, her hands balling the sheets.

I grunt in pleasure, hovering on the verge.

Her next moan sounds like she's in pain, and then her pussy spasms all around me, unleashing a chain reaction that makes me burst with the force of an atomic bomb.

Panting, she falls on the bed, face down, her every muscle relaxed.

I settle next to her, trying to catch my breath.

A sleepy post-coital haze hits me hard. Suppressing a yawn, I hug Lilly as if she were a teddy bear—in large part to make sure she's still here. Still real. To be certain that what's just happened between us was not a repeat of my recurring Lilly-themed wet dream.

But no. She is extremely real. The scrumptious smell of her hair, the luxurious warmth of her skin—my sleeping brain is simply incapable of such exquisite detail.

I finally lose my fight against that yawn, and she echoes it, then melts into my arms as her breathing becomes slower and more even.

She's asleep, is my last thought before I also pass out.

CHAPTER 26
LILLY

wake up and refuse to open my eyes. Like this, I can allow myself a second to believe that everything that happened was a dream. Then again, reality is hard to deny. For example, why am I sore in such a telling way? And what's with the hard masculinity in such close proximity to me—not to mention Bruce's signature scent?

I sigh. There's no helping it. I blink open my eyes, and surprise, surprise: I'm coiled around Bruce like a boa constrictor.

No more doubts. It really happened. I slept with my boss-nemesis, and it was beyond amazing.

Actually, it's not fair to view him as my nemesis anymore. My parents aren't upset with his bank. If anything, they sounded almost grateful for the deferral and what-not. Beyond that, he's working on a project that will help so many people, and—nearly as important to me—he genuinely loves Colossus.

Still, he *is* my boss. That's undeniable. Then again, it's not like this is a corporate environment where people might think I'm getting promotions for sleeping with him. I'm the only dog trainer here. And it's a temporary gig. Once Colossus learns everything that I have to teach, I'm gone.

My heart squeezes painfully. It doesn't like that idea even a little bit.

Must think of something else. For example, there was something that happened last night that was also not consistent with us being nemeses—Bruce seemed pretty upset at the idea of me getting hurt. Or was he just reluctant to get sued?

No. He's got enough money to get sued by a million of me.

Okay, so if we're not nemeses, what are we? A one-night stand? Probably. But, purely hypothetically, could we have more than an employee and boss relationship?

It's scary how easy that is to imagine. I mean, I don't trigger his misophonia, which seems huge. And the sex was out of this world—and I could tell he felt that too. We love the same dog and are crazy about *The Witcher*, even if in different formats. He's brutally honest, and I hate lies—which works well. I can't cook even under gunpoint, but he has a chef and likes to cook on top of that. Also—

The loud ringing of a phone plunges me right back to earth.

Bruce wakes up and reaches for the annoying thing.

"Hello?" His tone implies, "This had better be important."

"Here?" he asks. "Already?"

Hanging up, he curses creatively, then turns to me. "For some unfathomable reason, my parents took a red-eye. They've just passed the security gate."

Hmm… Does that mean now would be a bad time to ask him what last night meant to him? Assuming I can puzzle out what it meant to me first.

Bruce leaps off the bed and rushes to get dressed. I do the same. As I'm pulling on my nightie, it hits me. "I didn't walk Colossus in the middle of the night," I say guiltily. "He probably had an accident."

"No. I walked him," Bruce says as he buttons his shirt.

"You did?"

He nods. "I happened to wake up to go to the bathroom around three."

"You should've woken me. It's my job and all."

He gives me an inscrutable look. "You were sleeping very soundly."

"You watched me sleep?" And why is that hot instead of creepy?

"Anyway," he says. "If you had taken him, he might've thought you were trying to keep him away from my room and gotten upset again."

I bite my lip. "That's pretty plausible."

"I'm going to go greet my folks," Bruce says and heads for the door. Over his shoulder, he adds, "You might want to be wearing more by the time you meet them."

I blush. Wearing more—no shit. I turn to head to my room, but spot Colossus opening his eyes and wagging his tail.

"Hi," I say to him. "How did you sleep?"

He turns on his back, demanding a belly scratch.

The honor of petting me will cost you a cookie. No, two cookies. Actually, three would be even better.

He follows me to my room and watches with curiosity as I make myself presentable enough to meet Bruce's whole family. When I'm almost done, I notice Colossus sniffing the leg of my bed suspiciously.

"Oh, no, you don't," I say sternly and grab him. "Time for your walk."

As we sneak to the garage, I overhear voices exclaiming their greetings to Bruce. I hurry out before the puppy has an accident. When we're back, Colossus runs into the house and I follow—to the kitchen, as it turns out.

At the entrance to the kitchen, Colossus stops and cocks his head. I'm about to ask him what's wrong when I hear Bruce say, "No, we'll talk *after* breakfast. I have a meeting."

"Is this about our loud chewing again?" a petulant feminine voice asks, causing the dog to look at me with a confused expression. "I thought that with your income, you'd have fixed your issue... somehow."

"Your chewing isn't loud," Bruce says. "But I still can't tolerate it."

"But what about tonight?" The petulant tone increases. "We just flew all this way and—"

"Theodora, dearest, what's the point of arguing?" a booming man's voice chimes in. "You know how Bruce is about Mesopotamia."

Having heard enough, I pick up Colossus (who seems to be afraid of his grandparents) and waltz in. "I heard the word Mesopotamia," I say with a smile. "That's the cradle of civilization, isn't it?"

Bruce's eyes crinkle. "Lilly, meet my parents, Mr. and Mrs. Roxford, or as you'd insist on calling them: Ambrose and Theodora." Turning to his parents, he says, "Lilly is the dog trainer I told you about."

Merely a dog trainer? Fine. "Pleasure to meet you," I say and resist the odd urge to curtsy. I'm not sure names like Ambrose and Theodora sound any less formal than Mr. and Mrs. Roxford, but it's not like we're at the stage of our relationship where I could give them nicknames such as "A" and "The."

"The pleasure is ours," Theodora says and examines me like a pawn shop owner would a cubic zirconia wedding ring. "Though I have to say, you're smaller than we expected."

Is that the royal "we?"

"Mother," Bruce says sternly.

"It's fine," I say. "I'm aware of my fun-sized stature."

Theodora looks me up and down. "Petite women are very adorable and have so many advantages, like dating men of any height. But—"

"Seriously, Mom," Bruce says. "Enough."

What I want to know is, did she write a dissertation on the vertically challenged?

"We have a right to be concerned," Theodora states, and despite her use of "we," Ambrose steps away from her and looks extremely uncomfortable. He clearly doesn't want to be included in whatever she's talking about. "With her size," Theodora continues, "she might have trouble giving birth."

I almost choke on my tongue. "Giving birth? To what baby?" Is she insane enough to have poked holes in Bruce's condoms?

"A hypothetical one," Theodora says.

If you could get pregnant from blushing, I'd pee on a stick right here and now.

"The work I do for your son doesn't involve such hypotheticals," I say as evenly as I can. "And, if we're talking random hypotheticals, the situation you're describing is not a concern for me. Having a pelvis that is too narrow for childbirth has nothing to do with body size." When she arches a royal eyebrow, I add, "My cousin is a fertility expert, and she also likes to have unsolicited baby conversations."

"But"—Theodora darts her son a quick glance— "what if the hypothetical father is a large man?"

I think I'd prefer that Colossus bring one of my sex toys out here—even that would be less embarrassing than this conversation. "Baby size doesn't work like that," I say. "It's not the size when grown, but the size of the father and mother as a baby that matters."

"That's even worse," Theodora says. "My daughter, Angela, was a ten-pound behemoth."

Ambrose places a hand on his wife's shoulder. "Dear, you're forgetting that Bruce is a billionaire. He can get her the best medical care in the world, or hire a large-framed surrogate to carry the ginormous baby." Looking at me guiltily, he adds, "Hypothetically, I mean."

Theodora actually looks calmer, but it's unclear if it's her husband's words or hand that have done it. My desire to fall through the floor only increases.

"This conversation is over." Bruce strides over to the fridge and takes out three breakfasts: his own, Colossus's, and mine. "Here." He hands me the food. "I believe you have a long training session with Colossus coming up."

I'm both grateful and annoyed. It's good to be spared more face time with his parents, but at the same time, is he dismissing me because he hates their assumption that we're together?

Whatever. I snatch the food from his hands and stomp over to my room.

After our respective meals, I work with Colossus. First, I reinforce some of what he already knows, and then I teach him the "stay" command—which could've spared me the earlier kitchen encounter.

After a couple of hours, Colossus decides he's had enough and plops on his belly to chew a toy as far away from me as the locked room allows.

Fine. I can do my own thing. I pick up *The Witcher* to read, but my phone rings.

Huh. Like some gossip psychic, it's Aphrodite calling.

I debate picking up for a moment, then do so, hoping that talking to her will help me make sense of what's happened.

"Hi," I say timidly.

"You slut," Aphrodite exclaims. "You *already* slept with him?"

I sigh. "Yes."

Her response is a squeal so loud I have to pull the phone away from my ear lest I lose my hearing.

Colossus looks up from his chewing, confused.

That sounded like the squeaks of a Chihuahuan mouse. Are you getting a call from the homeland of my breed?

When she settles down, my cousin demands, "So? How was it?"

I sigh once again. "I'm officially ruined for anyone else."

There are notes of a stuck pig in Aphrodite's next squeal, and Colossus gives me another WTF look.

"Tell me everything," she says once she catches her breath. "*Everything.*"

Hesitating for only a moment, I proceed to tell her, taking pauses for squeals from time to time. I mention the kisses (yes, that's meant to be plural), the trip to the zoo, and as much as I'm comfortable sharing about the big event itself (yes, I did use protection). I finish with the encounter with his parents and then ask, "So… what do you think it means?"

"It means I was right," she says triumphantly.

"Yeah, yeah," I say with an eyeroll. "What do you think I mean to Bruce?"

She sucks in a breath. "What did he say this morning?"

"He didn't. His parents came early."

"Well, then, what do *you* think?" she says. "Considering that he took you on a date and then stormed your pink fortress."

I dart a questioning glance at my phone. "What date?"

"The zoo?"

"That was for the dog." Speaking of, I check on Colossus and find him napping.

"Sure. The dog." Her air quotes are audible. "Everyone takes Fido to the zoo… with the hot dog trainer. Was the romantic picnic for the dog too?"

Was it? Also, "hot dog trainer" makes it sound like I specialize in dachshunds.

"What about his dick?" she continues. "Was that for the dog?"

"That might've just been a guy taking advantage of an opportunity."

"Oh, come on. A good-looking billionaire? He can crook a finger and have opportunities lined up."

"So… you think it was a date?" I hate how hopeful I sound.

"For sure. And now that his parents approve of you, I bet he—"

"Wait, what?"

"His parents," she says. "Remember how you worried they would never let him date someone like you? Some bullshit about old money not mixing with white trash, which I still claim that *we* aren't?"

"I remember that," I say. "Just not the bit where anything's changed."

"Are you crazy?" she says. "Why else would his mother worry about you birthing his babies? And then his dad said, 'Just throw money at the problem,' as if you being preggers by their son were a given."

"Why does that make some warped kind of sense?" I ask, more to myself than to her.

"Because, my dear, you're going to be Mrs. Roxford," she says. "Please ask him if he's got a rich friend. A mere millionaire will be fine. Oh, and ask if I can tag along on your next helicopter ride."

"Do not tell your mom any of this," I say firmly. "Else I'm going to get a call from mine. Again."

"Not any of it?" She sounds like a kid with no gifts on Christmas morning.

"If you do, I'm never telling you anything again... and you can kiss the imaginary helicopter ride goodbye."

"Fine," she says grumpily. "But can I come after he confirms it *was* a date?"

"You'll come when I say you can," I state and hang up before she can beg me to change my mind.

Out of the corner of my eye, I spot Colossus sniffing around my bed, so I take him for his walk.

When we get back into the house, I order Colossus to stay.

Nope. Something—most likely the kitchen—is too interesting to resist.

Running after him, I hear voices in the kitchen and fully expect to bump into Ambrose and Theodora again, but that's not who is there. It's Angela, Bruce's sister—and, apparently, a carrier of the dreaded giant baby gene. Not that you can tell she was so big at birth. Currently, she's thin and small boned, and not *that* tall, at least compared to the rest of her family. Speaking of tall people, next to Angela is a man with a tan straight out of a bottle and a smile that doesn't touch his eyes—which are set too close together if you ask me.

"Peanut!" Angela exclaims when she spots the puppy.

"It's Colossus," I remind her.

"Ah, right," she says. "*Colossus*, please stay away from Champ. He's allergic."

Her boyfriend's name is Champ? Does he take it like one too?

"Hey," I say soothingly to Colossus, and when he looks at me, I take out a tiny cookie to emphasize my point. The gambit works. The dog stops before he can come into contact with Champ and runs to me. Good. The last thing we want is for the champ to melt, like the Wicked Witch.

"You go by Lilly, right?" Angela asks me as I grab the puppy.

"Yeah," I say. "And you?"

"You may call me Angela," she says, making it sound like the greatest act of charity known to man.

"Nice to meet you, Angela," I say. "In the flesh this time."

She nods. "You have very striking eyebrows."

"Thank you?"

She touches her own, much thinner ones. "Do you put Rogaine on them?"

"No," I say and resist frowning—because that would make said eyebrows move and thus bring even more attention to them. "Anyway, Colossus and I have a lot of training to do."

"Wait, before you go…" She turns to Champ. "Can you give us a moment?"

Champ gives me a weird look. "Sure. I'll go have a smoke." Turning, he heads out.

Why did he look at me like that? I glance at my reflection in the shiny microwave to make sure I'm not still wearing the Mohawk-like helmet.

Nope. I'm good.

Whatever. With Champ gone, I set Colossus back on the floor—something he clearly needed because he runs to his water bowl and gulps greedily, like he's been to the desert.

"So what's up?" I ask Angela as I refill his bowl.

She edges in front of me, blocking my way back to

Colossus. "Is something going on between you and my brother?"

Okay, whoa. This family is beyond nosy and blunt. Are the baby questions forthcoming? "Um… how is that any of your business?"

She wrinkles her tiny nose minutely. "My family *is* my business."

Huh. With her New York accent, that sounded like a line from a mafia movie.

"Why don't you ask Bruce?" I venture. *And please, please tell me what he says.*

She grimaces. "By now, you probably know that my brother can be difficult."

"Difficult? Bruce? Are we talking about the same man?"

Angela's smile is genuine—or so I assume. All that Botox makes it tricky to tell. "I have to admit, it would be fun to watch him date someone with such a smart mouth…"

"But?" I prod.

"But the two of you would be a bad idea," she says, managing to sound equal parts sincere and regretful.

Regardless, my hackles rise. "Oh? And why is that?"

She winces. "I thought it would be obvious."

"Not to me, it's not." Though I'm getting an inkling of where she's going, and I don't like it one bit. Even if I thought the same thing not too long ago.

She purses her lips. "When it comes to dating, like should be with like."

And there it is. If I wanted to maintain some

pretense of cordiality, I'd back off now, but I'm way past that point. "Care to explain?"

She glances at the puppy. "Well, to put it in terms you might understand, if the two of you were dogs, Bruce would be one of those show dogs with a pedigree going back to when his breed was first developed. You, on the other hand, would be closer to a mutt."

If I were a dog, I'd be full-on growling.

"Thanks for not saying I'd also be the runt of my litter," I retort sarcastically.

"Look, maybe that came out harsh, but—"

"It came out like something a female dog would say."

She flushes. "I—"

"Did you already ask her?" Theodora asks loudly, walking into the room.

She's in on this as well? So much for Aphrodite's delusions about this family accepting me.

"Not yet," Angela says.

Huh. So maybe—

"I'll ask her then," Theodora says and turns to me, her smile eerily reminiscent of her daughter's. "Will you help?"

"Help with what?"

"The party," Theodora says.

I draw back—and it's a miracle I don't step on poor Colossus. "What party?"

"The obvious one," Theodora says. "Given today."

"Um…" It's doubtful they'd want to celebrate the best sex of my life, but if not that, I'm at a loss.

Theodora frowns while Angela shakes her head and tsk-tsks.

"You seriously don't know?" Theodora peers at me with Bruce's blue eyes.

I shake my head.

"What today is?" Angela says pointedly.

When I shrug, Theodora finally takes pity on me. "It's Bruce's birthday."

CHAPTER 27
BRUCE

Just as I finish my Zoom call with my CTO about a breakthrough on the crypto, my dad walks in.

"Am I interrupting?" he asks.

I do have some emails to answer, but I wave for him to come in, in part because I don't spend that much quality time with my folks anymore, but also, it's a chance for me to disprove Lilly's workaholism accusations.

"Are you working on your birthday?" Dad asks.

"Are you going to call me a workaholic?" I retort.

Dad smiles. "I'm going to say I'm proud of your work ethic."

Yeah, and since I learned it from him, what else is he supposed to say?

"So…" Dad sits down. "Your girlfriend is nice."

I should've told him about the emails after all. "Are

you designating Lilly as my girlfriend, or are we talking about someone else?"

Dad's smile widens to Joker levels. "Lilly."

"Did you ask *her* if she's okay with the girlfriend moniker?" Even if she considered it this morning, she's bound to dismiss the idea as insane after that baby conversation with Mom.

Reading something in my expression, Dad says, "Don't be mad at your mother. After all... your Lilly *is* awfully small."

My Lilly. I do like the sound of that.

A lot.

But her perky body is not too small. It's pure perfection—and is henceforth my type, even though I always thought I didn't have a type. Not that I plan to tell any of this to my father. It was bad enough sitting through his version of "the birds and the bees" when I was five, and him laughing when I asked what I still think was a reasonable question: "Does it hurt?"

I mean, it hurts most women the first time, so—

"You're the opposite of small," Dad continues. "So I hope things can work for you two in that department."

"What are you, twelve?" I demand. What I don't plan to tell him is that things *did* work out, better than I could've ever imagined. It was mind-blowing. The best I—

"I'm sorry," Dad says with visible contrition. "Oh, and in my defense, I should mention I didn't come here to discuss your love life."

"No?" I don't even bother correcting the "love life" bit.

"The female members of the family are scheming about a party."

I grit my teeth. "Birthday?"

Dad nods.

"What's the thought process there? I hated the first thirty-four birthdays, but this year will magically be different?"

"You liked your fifth birthday party," Dad says.

Maybe. There was a clown at that one, and no food that I can recall. But apart from that one exception, I loathe all events where eating is a central theme—and especially the evil trinity: Thanksgiving, Christmas, and birthdays.

"Why didn't you stop them?" I demand.

Dad snorts. "If they can be stopped, why don't you go ahead and do it?"

He's right.

I frantically run through various excuses in my head.

A work emergency? Weak.

Appendicitis? No, they'd follow me to the hospital.

Explosive diarrhea?

Fuck.

Why haven't I found myself a body double—like Saddam Hussein, Kim Jong-un, and Keanu Reeves?

I guess there's no helping it. To stay sane, I'll have to use industrial-strength earplugs or high-end noise cancelation headphones because there's no way around it.

I'll have to soldier through yet another fucking birthday party.

CHAPTER 28
LILLY

"It's his birthday?" I look at each woman in turn. "He hasn't said a word about it." Then again, why would he tell his humble employee such personal details, right? I'm lucky he—

"Don't feel bad," Theodora says. "When it comes to holidays, Bruce is the family Grinch."

"But we think he secretly likes us fussing over him," Angela says. "When we don't make him celebrate, he just works extra hours." She wrinkles her perfect nose. "I don't think he has ever treated himself to anything more than an extra-vigorous workout on his birthday."

I can totally see that. "But don't people eat at parties?" I ask, and feel silly doing so. "And drink?"

"Well, yeah," Angela says. "And you're right. That may be part of the reason for the Grinchness."

"Part? Might be?" I can't believe this. "Bruce has misophonia. The sounds of eating and drinking are triggers."

Theodora clears her throat. "We can have tiny hors d'oeuvres at the party, something people can swallow whole."

"And shots," Angela says. "Tiny ones that people can down without making too much sound."

Bruce wasn't exaggerating when he said his family does not respect his condition.

"No one will be able to eat or drink in front of Bruce anymore," I decree. When they look at me questioningly, I less confidently add, "I trained Colossus to stop anyone from trying."

They both look at me like I've grown horns, but neither asks how a tiny Chihuahua is supposed to stop humans from eating or drinking.

"Having said that," I add. "Why not set up two eating stations: one just for Bruce and another for everyone else, out of Bruce's earshot? And two bars set up similarly."

"That's very smart," Theodora says. "We'll do it that way."

"We can also blast the music loudly," I say. "Or better yet, have a headphones party."

"Let's do the second idea," Angela says. "Bruce wears headphones at most eating events anyway, and this way, he won't look like he's lacking social graces."

Him wearing headphones doesn't make *him* look like he lacks social graces. That honor belongs to whoever eats or drinks in front of him after learning about his condition.

"That's settled then," Theodora says. "I'll invite his

friends and hire a DJ who can set up the headphones thing."

Angela claps her hands excitedly. The party is clearly more for her than for Bruce. "We also need a theme."

"How about *The Witcher*?" I blurt.

"The what?" they ask in unison.

How could they not know this? "That's his favorite book series."

Theodora looks at Angela meaningfully, then focuses on me. "He told you that?"

I blush. "I happen to like a video game based on said series, and we happened to talk about it."

"Common interests," Theodora says approvingly. "Then tell us, if we want *that* to be the party theme, what should we do?"

I shrug. "Can you find us some outfits that resemble those worn in medieval Eastern Europe?"

Angela gives me a "well, duh" look.

"We can have the men wear swords," I say, getting into the spirit of things. "And the women can get extra dolled up to resemble the sorceresses of that world." In *The Witcher*, the sorceresses use magic to look their best, not unlike this mother and daughter who use plastic surgery, so they will fit their roles well.

"What else?" Angela asks.

"Can you hire a bard?" I suggest.

Angela arches her as-yet-unRogained eyebrow. "A bard?"

"It's like a minstrel," I explain. "Think, a guy dressed

in a dandy version of the clothing everyone will be wearing, while spouting poetry and playing a lute."

"Ah, sure," Angela says. "That should be easy."

It should be? I guess rich people have access to bards—and probably get them at the same supermarket where they go to buy creepy masks and prostitutes for their *Eyes Wide Shut*-esque parties.

"The dog should have an outfit," Theodora says. "Any ideas?"

I grin. "He can be a werewolf—Chihuahua by day, cursed beast by night."

Theodora and Angela look down at the little ball of fluff dubiously. Are they wondering if werewolf powers are how he'll keep people eating and drinking away from Bruce?

"Any other option?" Theodora asks.

"He can be a horse," I say reluctantly. What I don't add is that I used this idea with my dog for many a Halloween, or that my dog was named after the Witcher's mount.

"That should be easier on such short notice," Theodora says.

Oh? So there *are* limits to the *Eyes Wide Shut* supermarket. Good to know.

"All right," Angela says. "We've got lots to do, so we'd better get started."

"May I have your number?" Theodora asks me. "In case I have questions regarding the theme?"

I enter my phone number into her contacts, then take Colossus for another walk.

Outside, I spot Champ, who's probably smoking his second carton of cigarettes at this point.

"Mad Max cosplay?" he asks with a smirk, pointing at my headgear. "You also need a bra with spikes." With that, he ogles my boobs as if picturing said getup.

"So clever," I say through gritted teeth. "I almost forgot how stupid Bruce makes me look on these walks."

"Well, who can blame the guy." Champ tosses his cigarette on the ground. "If you worked for me, I'd also have you wear special outfits."

Ew. "Easy there, Champ. Your girlfriend is two feet away."

"It was just a fucking joke." Champ stomps on his cigarette, turns around, and skedaddles.

Wow. When Angela said that "like should be with like," *he* is who she thinks is her equal?

Colossus walks over to sniff the cigarette butt, so I pull him away in case he decides to eat it.

After the walk, I train Colossus, all the while fighting the giddiness I feel whenever I picture Bruce's Witcher-themed birthday party. From time to time, Theodora texts to ask me for more detailed suggestions about the theme, and at one point, she informs me of something that I obviously knew long ago—that *The Witcher* is also a TV show on Netflix, one that stars, and I quote, "the super-scrumptious, super-gorgeous Superman that is Henry Cavill."

I haven't seen it yet, I reply.

Maybe you can watch it with Bruce? Theodora suggests.

Who knows? I text back and wonder if she realizes she came very close to suggesting her son and I Netflix and chill.

An hour after lunch, I get one more text from Theodora:

Which of these outfits do you like?

Images flood my phone, and the choices are numerous, but I gravitate toward the black options because that is the color of choice of my favorite female character in the game, Yennefer of Vengerberg.

After a quick deliberation, I text Theodora my selections: tall boots, a cloak, a belt, a pair of long gloves, breeches, a fur collar, and last but not least, a girdle.

What size? she asks.

When I tell her, there's a pause, and then she replies with:

We're lucky this place tailors to both adults and kids.

Great. Are we back on the topic of my diminutive size?

To my relief, Theodora leaves me alone after that text, at least until she and Angela return and knock on my bedroom door. When I open it, Theodora thrusts a bunch of shopping bags into my hands.

"How much do I owe you?" I ask.

"Nothing," Theodora says graciously.

Angela nods. "We love the theme idea so much we feel like we owe *you.*"

All I did was tell them something they should've known, but okay.

"The party will start in three hours, in the ballroom," Angela says. "I hope that's enough time for you to get ready."

Was that a diss in the vein of, "You're so ugly it will take you extra-long to cover it all up?"

"Just three hours?" Theodora looks at her watch with a horrified expression. "Is it too late to move everything back? There's no way I'll be ready in time."

"No," Angela says. "Dad has contrived some excuse to bring Bruce into that room at that exact time. If the time changes, Bruce could get suspicious."

"I'll have to hurry then," Theodora says. "See you."

As her mother rushes away, Angela stays behind for some reason.

Oh, no. Am I about to get another lecture on my unsuitability for her brother? Maybe this time I'll be compared to a lowly donut hole and he to a champagne cake?

"I'd better run too. I take even longer to get ready than Mom," Angela says but doesn't move.

I sigh. "What is it now?"

She almost imperceptibly shifts from one high heel onto the other. "Thank you. I appreciate your help with this party."

Leaving me gaping, she clickity-clacks away.

"What was that about?" I ask Colossus.

He cocks his head.

If I were that good at understanding humans, I'd get you all to hand me cookies every second of every day.

———

Dressed in my Yennefer outfit, I arrive at the ballroom a few minutes early. Colossus is with me, looking like the smallest pony in the history of equines.

Johnny greets us at the entrance, dressed like a bard.

I smile at him. "It's like your mustache has waited its entire existence for this night."

With a pleased blush, Johnny twirls said mustache expertly. "These are for you." He hands me a pair of earbuds.

In order to expose my ears, I have to push back the jet-black locks of my wig. Once the buds are in, I hear soft lute music, just like I would in a tavern in Novigrad, my favorite city in the game.

Nice.

I look around.

The decorations are spot on; I wouldn't be surprised to learn that Theodora and Angela hired a set designer. The ballroom reminds me of Kaer Morhen, the ancient castle where all the Witchers train.

Spotting Bruce's father at what must be a no-Bruce food station, I head over and check the selection.

Wow. Even the hors d'oeuvres are on theme, with labels like "mutton slider" and "wyvern tartar." As I fix myself a plate of different cheeses and fruits, I grab some cucumber for Colossus—who gobbles it desperately despite the fact that he ate his dinner on the way here.

Ambrose accidentally bangs his scabbard on the side of the table. "You think Bruce will like all this?"

"I'm as big a fan of this world as he is," I say. "And I love it."

After quickly finishing my food in the designated area, I come out to check the gathering crowd.

Everyone is dressed in appropriate outfits, and I recognize Bob the chef, Prudence the housekeeper, the gardener whatever-his-name-is, and some security guards. Then a crowd of familiar folks walks in, also dressed up, and it takes me a second to remember that they're from that nearby branch of Bruce's bank—the very ones who helped in Colossus's socialization.

Recognizing the smell of his human acquaintances, Colossus runs off to greet them—or check if they have treats.

Angela, Angela's boyfriend, and Theodora walk in. Both women make excellent fellow sorceresses, while Champ looks like a Nilfgaardian court jester. They join Ambrose, who's dressed as a king, most likely Radovid V the Stern.

"He's coming," Johnny says and nervously twirls his mustache. "Get ready."

I watch the entrance curiously.

Bruce steps in, looking like an anachronism in his modern clothes.

"Surprise!" we all shout. "Happy birthday!"

Eye widening, Bruce looks around, a bit shell-shocked.

Ambrose strides over to his son and thrusts a bundle of clothing into his hands. "Please put this on and come back," he says, sounding vaguely apologetic. "This party has a theme."

Colossus runs over to Bruce and wags his tail.

Peering at the horse outfit, Bruce graces us all with one of his rare smiles. "Are you mini-Roach?"

The puppy wags his tail harder.

I don't care what you call me, so long as there's a cookie in it for me.

"Well, let's go," Bruce says to the dog, and they depart together.

I head over to the no-Bruce bar and order a shot of vodka. When I'm back on the dance floor, Bruce and Colossus return.

Holy Anubis. I should've guessed Angela and Theodora would end up doing this, yet I find myself unprepared and in need of new panties.

Already broad-shouldered by nature, Bruce looks huge with the signature armor shoulder plates of his costume. And given the gray wig, the two swords on his broad back, and the signature wolf pendant on his neck, there can be no doubt about who he is: Geralt of Rivia, or as everyone thinks of him, the Witcher.

CHAPTER 29
BRUCE

Even though I expected a surprise party, the theme threw me for a loop, so my shock was genuine.

Later, as I was changing, I got a chance to process everything and realized that for the first time, I might actually enjoy my stupid birthday party, or at least find it easier to tolerate. It also didn't take long for me to figure out whom I have to thank for this. After all, she's as big a fan of this universe as I am.

Which is why, when Colossus and I step back into the ballroom, I seek Lilly in the crowd.

It takes me a few moments on account of all the outfits, but once I focus on height (or lack thereof) and eyebrows (or an abundance thereof), I locate her—and feel my eyes begin to bulge, like those of a cartoon wolf, which is fitting given the pendant on my neck.

She looks sexy as hell—and of course, she's dressed as my character's love interest.

Walking over to her, I pull out the earbuds from under my wig and say hi.

She rids herself of her buds and sings "Happy Birthday" in that special way made famous by Marilyn Monroe, just replacing "Mr. President" with "Mr. Roxford."

As I listen, I wonder how wrong it would be if I threw her over my shoulder and ran to my bedroom. Would everyone think it's part of the cosplay? Probably not, so I'd better behave.

"Thank you." I gesture around. "Whoever came up with the Witcher theme is a genius."

She bats her eyelashes at me coquettishly. "I wonder who she was?"

I shrug theatrically. "I'm picturing someone beautiful. Thoughtful. Probably great with dogs."

There it is, the blush I was trying my best to generate. "Have you eaten?" She points to the corner away from everyone. "That's the station for you to eat at, which is separate from everyone else's."

I step closer. "Your idea?"

Looking up at me, she nods.

I lean down. "You're amazing."

She rises on her tiptoes. "It was my pleasure."

Are we still talking about this party?

Doesn't matter.

I'm tasting those lips again.

I lean in another inch, but just as I'm about to kiss Lilly, a hand taps my shoulder.

Turning, I prepare to slice the interrupter with one

of my swords, but it turns out to be my mom, so I have to settle for a glare. "What?"

"The two of you should have the first dance," Mom declares.

I look from her to Lilly. "Do birthdays have first dances?" I always thought it was a wedding thing.

"It's because of your outfits," Mom says lamely. "The Witcher must dance with his sorceress."

Lilly points at Gertrude, who's wearing a red wig. "That's Triss Marigold. In the game, romancing *her* leads to a simpler and more stable life."

"No spoilers." I pop my earbuds back in. "Not that I would have chosen anyone but Yennefer regardless of what you said."

Slow music plays in my ears, and I extend my hand to Lilly. She also inserts her buds, then takes my hand, and I lead her into the middle of the dance floor as everyone looks on.

"I'm glad your swords are behind your back," Lilly whispers loudly enough for me to hear through the earbuds. "If you were wearing them on your belt, I'd be at risk of getting stabbed."

"You're still at risk." Feeling like a kid at prom, I dart a glance at my tightening pants.

Blushing in a very un-Yennefer fashion, Lilly takes my proffered hands and I pull her close, moving to the music in a ballroom-dance style since I have no clue how dancing is supposed to look in the Witcher world.

Having Lilly near me is intoxicating. She looks up at me demurely, is soft in all the right places, and her delicate scent of cherries, incense, and roses makes my head spin.

Fuck. My sword situation becomes more obvious—and given how her eyes widen, she notices.

The music stops.

I bow. "You're a great dancer."

"Why, thank you." She curtsies. "How about you eat and drink, and then we do it again?"

"It's a date," I say and head over to the station she set up for me. Though, truth be told, I'm not hungry or thirsty anymore...

Or at least, not for food.

CHAPTER 30
LILLY

That dance was hot, and not just because it tapped into my fantasies involving the Witcher. It was much more due to Bruce, who, as of recently, has become a source of so many more fantasies than a video game character could ever elicit.

I fan myself with my palm, wishing my outfit included a fan or a fly swatter. Nope. Still hot and bothered. Muting the music, I even out my breath, then walk over to the bar and get myself a glass of water with plenty of ice.

Even the cold drink doesn't help. Maybe sneaking an ice cube into my panties would work better, but it doesn't seem like the best idea when surrounded by so many people.

"Your Majesty," I suddenly overhear Theodora whisper theatrically. "Any chance we can sneak out and visit our quarters while no one is looking?"

I assume she's speaking to Ambrose, and that I'm not the only one finding these outfits to be an aphrodisiac. Also, I'd better be careful with what I say tonight. When the music is muted, the earbuds don't block much sound.

"Yes, wench," Ambrose replies before I can resume the music and thus muffle the unwelcome TMI. "You may receive the honor of servicing your king very soon."

I don't hear what Bruce's mom replies with because the music in my headphones blissfully drowns it out, but I still need bleach for my brain.

Putting some distance between myself and Bruce's parental units, I step out of the bar area and run smack into Champ.

Yuck. I feel parts of him brush my body and am assaulted by his breath—a horrible mixture of cigarettes, garlic, vodka, and coffee.

I swiftly back away. On the bright side, I don't need that cold shower anymore.

Champ leers at me, unleashing more of the breath. "Would the magic lady like to dance?"

I breathe through my mouth. "No. Thank you."

He frowns. "Why not?"

"She only dances with me," Bruce growls threateningly from behind me, startling both me and Champ.

Champ raises his hands. "It's just a dance. Sheesh."

"We're very dedicated to the theme," I say. "And his character would only dance with mine, and vice versa."

Rolling his eyes in a girly fashion, Champ turns on his heel and strides away.

"Thanks," I mouth to Bruce.

"You can thank me with a dance," Bruce replies and extends his hands to me, just like earlier.

Here we go. My panties are in trouble again.

I accept his hands, and he pulls me near him expertly, enveloping me in his body heat.

The music is a little faster this time, but it's nothing compared to my frantic heartbeat.

His arm cradles my back, gently guiding me to the rhythm.

Did whoever invent dancing realize how sex-like it is?

I gasp with every step, my pushed-up breasts heaving. Then Bruce's eyes meet mine, and there's not a hint of the usual ice in their blue depths. Instead, they remind me of the Caribbean Sea, where I'd gladly skinny dip.

The music turns, and Bruce gives me a gentle dip to the beat. I nearly swoon.

"You're a very good dancer," Bruce murmurs into my ear when the song stops.

"Me? You're the one who did all the work."

He smiles. "You underestimate your sense of rhythm."

Do I, or do I have other, more primal things on my mind?

"I want to thank you again," he says. "When it comes

to birthday presents, I'm hard to satisfy, but you did so today."

I blame the words "hard" and "satisfy" for what I blurt out next, which is, "This party isn't my gift."

His eyes gleam. "It's not?"

Blushing, I say, "What do you think of spending the night with Yennefer of Vengerberg?"

Gah. How much have I drunk? I'm not usually so brave.

He shakes his head, and my heart nearly stops. "I don't want Yennefer of Vengerberg," he murmurs. "Not when I can have Lilly Johnson."

The breath I didn't realize I was holding whooshes out of my lungs. I open my mouth to talk logistics, but Bruce's expression turns pained.

I spin around.

Champ is behind me, chewing a mutton slider with his mouth open, like a fucking caveman.

"What the hell?" I say sternly. "You're supposed to eat in the designated area."

"The dog was there." Champ waves with the slider and takes another bite.

Speaking of the dog, Colossus is running our way, which proves Champ didn't really accomplish anything by leaving, not that I buy his explanation. My theory is that he wants some petty revenge on Bruce for not letting him dance with me.

Feeling beyond annoyed, I put my hand to my temple and look meaningfully at the puppy.

Being the good boy that he is, Colossus barks,

loudly.

Champ's hand flies to his chest, and he takes a backward step just in time to trip over Johnny's foot (or maybe mustache).

Arms flailing, Champ plops on his ass, the leftover sandwich flying in Colossus's direction.

Without so much as a blink, the dog devours the sandwich—no doubt thinking that's his treat for barking on command.

"What was in that sandwich?" I demand.

"That's what you're worried about?" Champ asks and tries to turn with a groan.

"Answer her," Bruce barks.

The chef runs over and rattles off a list of ingredients. They sound mostly dog safe, so I relax a bit. I'll still need to keep an eye on the puppy, in case the overeating makes him sick, but I'm guessing the insatiable little creature will be okay. Speaking of okay...

"Are you hurt?" I ask Champ, who's still on the floor. If he broke his coccyx bone, I'd feel a little guilty.

Without any words of sympathy, Bruce extends his hand to Champ, who takes it and rises to his feet with another groan.

"This is the fucking dog's fault," he mutters, brushing himself off. "I'm allergic."

"Since when do allergies make you fall on your ass?" Bruce asks.

Champ fake-sneezes in reply and scurries away, clearly unhurt.

"Good boy," Bruce says to Colossus.

The puppy wags his tail.

If you thought I was a good boy for eating that sandwich, just wait until you see my highly refined cookie-eating skills.

"He might need the bathroom after such a big meal," I tell Bruce. "Colossus, I mean, but maybe Champ too."

"How about we take him together?" Bruce suggests.

And be alone. Yes, please. But wait. I look around. "What about the party?"

Bruce shrugs. "I've lasted longer here than at any other event I've been to. Thanks to you."

"Okay then." I grab the puppy. "Let's go."

We stroll toward the garage in companionable silence, and by the time we get there, Colossus is napping in my arms. Food coma got him.

"I almost feel bad for waking him," I whisper to Bruce.

Seeing the cute, sleepy face, he smiles. "I wonder why he's so tired."

"The party," I say. "All the smells and the people and the food. It's a lot for a tiny guy."

"Should we take him back to bed?" he asks.

I shake my head. "He'll have an accident for sure."

Bruce hands me the dog's harness, and I suit him up, then reach for my punky headgear.

"You won't need that," Bruce says.

"It's dark out," I say. "Won't I be at risk for an owl attack?"

Bruce takes out one of his swords from behind his back. "Let the feathery fuckers try. I'll slice them in two."

I attach the leash to Colossus's harness. "Is that your steel or silver blade?"

He looks at it more closely. "Silver. I should probably handle an owl with steel."

"Yeah. Silver is for monsters, and I don't think owls qualify."

"Speaking of *The Witcher*," Bruce says as we step into the cool night air. "My mother told me something interesting."

"She did?" Didn't she just learn about the series from me today?

"There's a TV show on Netflix based on *The Witcher*."

Oh. "You didn't already know that?"

He shakes his head.

Butterflies flutter in my stomach as I ask, "Did you want to watch it?"

"With you," he says.

The fluttering becomes full-on flapping, and the butterflies grow into predatory owls. "I'd like that."

"Not that it could be as good as the books," Bruce says.

"Or the third game," I add.

"If we hate it, at least we'll hate it together."

"Yeah," I say. "The key is to chill as we watch."

And... the drunken bravery keeps going, needlessly in this case, as he's already agreed to accept me as a gift.

He grins. "As in, Netflix and chill?"

I grin back, even as my face turns hot. "You get me."

His expression turns serious. I think he must

realize how romantic this moment is. We've got gorgeous surroundings around us, the stars and the moon in the clear sky above, and last but not least, we're dressed in sexy outfits that complement each other.

The same thoughts must be going through his head because he pulls me to him and our lips lock.

The awe-inspiring world around us completely disappears, and all that's left are Bruce's lips, his clever tongue, his strong arms on my ass, the whine—

Wait. Whine?

I grudgingly pull away and see the source of the whine. It's Colossus. He's standing on his hind legs and tapping Bruce with his front paws—as if begging to be picked up.

"Huh," I say. "Roach used to do something like this. He'd get between me and anyone I tried kissing."

"He was a smart dog then," Bruce says. "I'm the only person you should be kissing."

Wow. "I didn't know you then."

Bruce picks up Colossus and gets his face licked. "Do you think he just wanted attention, was jealous, or"—he chuckles—"was protecting me from a perceived attack?"

I shrug. "It looks more like he smelled oxytocin in the air and got curious about it. Maybe even wanted some too—hence the licking of your face." Lucky little bugger. I'm certainly a little jealous of that.

He puts the dog back on the ground. "If this becomes a problem, can you teach him not to butt in?"

"Sure," I say, my breathing speeding up. "We'd have to kiss a whole bunch as part of that training."

He smirks. "That can be arranged."

Okay. Here, right now, is my chance to ask him what is going on between us, but then again, it's his birthday, and if the conversation goes south, I will have ruined it.

Yeah. Postponing the talk. Maybe I'm not so brave after all.

"You think he's done?" Bruce asks after Colossus doesn't lift a leg on a bush that's so perfect for that purpose even I'm tempted to pee on it.

"Oh, yeah," I say. "The tank is empty. Let's go back."

And if it means we end up in Bruce's bedroom sooner, all the better.

Without discussing it, we half-run on the way back —which doesn't help my already-crazy heartbeat. On the way to the bedroom, the puppy falls asleep in my arms again, so I deposit him very gently into his bed when we get there and thank Anubis he didn't wake up.

Now what? I'm not sure if the last remnants of alcohol have left my system or if it's the reality of the bedroom, but I'm feeling a lot less brazen all of a sudden, which is why I blush as I ask, "Should we watch the TV show?"

Eyes gleaming hungrily, Bruce responds by lifting me off my feet and carrying me to the bed.

Oh, my. He pulls off each of my long boots, then dispenses with my breeches and girdle before finally peeling off my panties.

"Wow," Bruce purrs. "I've been dreaming about tasting you."

I turn crimson, but I don't fight it when he spreads my legs. The birthday boy can eat anything he wants—and as loudly as he wants since I'm not the one with misophonia.

He starts with featherlight kisses around my clit—an act of pure evil because it makes me want him *on* my clit.

As if psychically in tune with my desires, Bruce kisses where I so desperately want, barely touching it at first, then harder, ending in a solid smooch that makes my fists ball into the sheets.

He escalates his ministrations to a tiny lick.

A moan escapes from somewhere deep inside me.

I'm not sure how, but I feel his satisfied smirk against my pussy, followed by a stronger lick.

Yes. Please. Like that.

I must yell that out loud, or he's being a psychic again, because his next dozen or so licks are the same, and it's pure bliss. An orgasm begins to coil inside me as an unbidden moan escapes my lips.

Encouraged, Bruce does something I've never felt before—and redefines the term "clever tongue" in the process. It feels as though he's somehow enveloped my clit with his tongue.

With a cry, I break into little pieces of pleasure, then reconstitute back around his genius tongue.

"Your turn," I gasp when my senses return.

Now that I think about it, we should've started with him—it's his birthday and all.

In a move straight out of *Magic Mike*, Bruce rips his pants off, unleashing Titan.

"Commando?" I gently brush the tips of my fingers along his impressive length. "That's on theme."

"No," he grunts. "The real Geralt would wear braies."

"Hush." I give the tip of Titan a light kiss, tasting the ocean sweetness of Bruce's precum.

He leans back against the headboard, but that doesn't relax the knotted muscles in his legs, nor the V-shaped gorgeousness around his chiseled sixpack.

I take Titan in my mouth. It's harder than steel, yet warm and wonderfully velvety, just begging to be sucked and licked.

I can't believe I'm so turned on after he's just made me come. Unable to help myself, I sneak my hand between my legs, desperate to satiate the growing need.

"Fuck," Bruce growls as I give him an ice-cream lick. "You're unbelievable."

Oh, yeah? I slide Titan deep into my throat until I feel it all the way in my spleen. My own orgasm is almost here, and my resulting moan reverberates in his cock.

Groaning in pleasure, Bruce strokes my back—which just urges me to nudge him deeper and touch myself harder, more desperately.

"I want to be inside you," Bruce demands just as my orgasm is about to crest.

My mind is too sex-muddled to reply, so I just watch as Bruce lays me on the bed and sheaths Titan: first into the condom, then into me.

Eyes rolling into the back of my head, I rake Bruce's back as my orgasm finally makes landfall—all over his cock.

"Good girl," he croons, then splays my arms above my head and interlaces our fingers. "Now I want you to give me another one." He accompanies his demand with a thrust.

If I *could* speak at the moment, I'd say that I may be able to squeeze out one more, provided he keeps looking into my eyes like that. Like I'm the center of his universe.

He thrusts into me harder and captures my moan with his mouth. He feels so amazing inside me I could scream, but his scorching kiss prevents me from doing so.

His thrusts turn more frantic, and his tongue seems to be echoing what his pelvis is doing as he hungrily ravishes my mouth. Then he tenses, pulling away from the kiss to groan out loud, and I feel him grow impossibly hard inside me as he reaches his release.

That's it. With a choked cry, I come, and the ecstasy goes on for what feels like an eternity.

Whew. It's a good thing I'm on my back because I don't think I have the energy to do anything but sink into the mattress. My every muscle has jellified.

He sprawls next to me, his breathing equally ragged. "I can't believe the dog slept through all that."

I force my facial muscles to function. "I know, right?"

"Stay with me tonight," he murmurs, kissing my eyebrow.

I nod sleepily. "Unless you're volunteering to carry me to my room, that's the only option available."

And with that, I let myself pass out.

CHAPTER 31
BRUCE

I wake up in the middle of the night with Lilly wrapped around me like a fluffy-eyebrowed blanket. The images of what I did to her last night rush in, hardening my dick.

She was magnificent again—and yesterday was somehow one of the best days of my life, despite it being a dreaded birthday.

Since I can't fathom waking her up, I get up and take the puppy for a walk myself.

As we stroll through the moonlit grounds, I realize I may need to reevaluate a few things when it comes to Lilly. For one thing, regardless of our size difference, we are a perfect fit, sexually speaking. I've never had a woman feel so custom made for me.

I may also have to reconsider my stance on dating an employee. It's not optimal, for sure, but at least this isn't a corporate setting. That has to make it better, right?

One thing is for sure: the age gap isn't something to worry about. I haven't seen her take a single selfie, express any desire to dance in nightclubs, or squeal over Justin Bieber.

By the time I put Colossus back into his bed and rejoin Lilly, I decide that I'm going to talk to her about making whatever is going on between us official. But when? After the cryptocurrency project? That now seems too far.

No. I'll talk to her as soon as my parents leave.

CHAPTER 32
LILLY

There's movement in the bed, so I grumpily open an eye.

"Morning," Bruce murmurs.

"Shit." I open the second eye. "Did I brush my teeth last night?"

He snorts. "We didn't shower either—something I'm about to rectify."

He throws off his part of the blanket, and the sight of him naked is like mainlining espresso—especially since Titan is hard for some unfathomable reason.

If I didn't feel super gross, I'd jump him.

Wait. Did he just invite *me* into that shower with him?

Before I can sleuth out the answer, I hear the pitter-patter of tiny claws on the hardwood floor, followed by the tapping of paws on the mattress.

Bruce grins. "Guess who's awake too?"

I lean off the bed and come eye to eye with

Colossus—who wags his tail like it's his whole purpose in life before plopping onto his back.

Belly rub. Now. Chop-chop. It's been ages since I got some TLC.

I scratch the proffered belly with a wide grin.

"You've got him, right?" Bruce asks, still mouthwateringly naked. "I have a meeting in a few minutes."

"Yeah," I say with a sigh and watch the marvel that is Bruce's muscled ass walk away.

As soon as he's out of sight, I throw on my sorceress outfit, grab the puppy, and rush to my room, feeling like I'm doing the walk of shame as I go.

"Here." I give Colossus some dehydrated sweet potato chews the chef created.

As the dog works on the treat, I do my morning routine and ponder what's quickly becoming a bigger and bigger question.

What is going on between me and Bruce?

I know what it's *not* anymore—a one-night stand. Is there such a thing as a two-night stand? No idea, and I know I should talk to him about this, but I'm not sure how to bring it up.

Maybe I'll find the courage later today?

For now, I need to take the dog for a walk.

———

When Colossus and I return, Bruce is about to leave with his family to play golf.

"Why don't you join us?" Theodora asks.

I shake my head, smiling politely. "Colossus and I have a lot of training to do."

Is that disappointment on Bruce's face? Regardless, the puppy and I haven't had breakfast either—and more importantly, I don't want to intrude on Bruce's family time.

As promised, I work with my charge the whole day, stopping only for meals, and tragically, without bumping into Bruce even once.

When it's time to go to sleep, I take a shower, brush my teeth, and shave my legs and other necessary places before throwing on the sexiest pajamas I own: a tiny nightie. Then, properly primped, I take Colossus to his bed.

When we enter, the lights are on and Bruce isn't there, but I spot something new.

A TV sticking out of the foot of the bed. Or maybe it's not new? Maybe all Bruce needs to do is press a button and the TV slides out from somewhere.

Bruce steps out of his bathroom, wearing a robe. "We're all set to watch the show. Assuming you still want to."

Do I want some Netflix and chill? With him? Doesn't my outfit answer that for me?

"What about this one?" I lift Colossus.

Bruce walks over and rubs his fur child's belly. "How about we do some of that training we talked about?"

"You mean his reaction to kissing?" I ask, doing my best not to jump up and down in my excitement.

Bruce nods, grabs the puppy, and brings him to the bed.

Colossus plops down between Bruce's legs and seems to pass out.

"Let's see," Bruce says, then grabs me and gives me a loud kiss that would knock my socks (and panties) off —if I were wearing any.

Upon hearing the smooch, Colossus turns to investigate but then lies back down.

"He's tired," I say with a grin. "I think we can use this to our advantage."

With that, I kiss Bruce again.

We get a glance from the dog, but that's it.

On the next kiss, Colossus doesn't even bother getting up, so I take him to his bed.

"TV?" Bruce asks.

"Let's makes sure he's asleep," I say and loudly kiss Bruce.

When the dog doesn't react, Bruce kisses my neck, then my collarbone, and by the time he's sucking my nipple, I forget all about TV.

The next day passes in a similar manner. I wake up in Bruce's bed, he splits his day between work and his family, and I meet him in his room to watch *The Witcher*. Which is really just code for lots and lots of sex, as no TV gets watched. The only issue is that I still haven't found a way to bring up the big question.

What exactly is going on with us?

Also, shouldn't he bring it up at some point? Why is this on me? Or is this just a meaningless fling for him and not worthy of discussion?

I push the thought away, and we spend the following day the same way—except we *do* finally get to watch some fifteen minutes of *The Witcher* before Bruce fucks my brains out once again.

Still no discussion of anything.

Alrighty then.

The next day, I learn that his family is going to stay for another week—a week that starts off in much the same vein, with only sporadic watching of *The Witcher* and lots of orgasms for me. By now, I've had more orgasms with Bruce than in all of my previous relationships combined.

By day six, I'm mad at myself for not braving the conversation, but even madder at Bruce for not sparing me the need to do so.

I'm so pissed at him that I'm actually rehearsing the possible things I'll say to him in chastisement as I walk with Colossus in the morning. Every other morning before today, I played out the different versions of the "what's going on between us" talk instead, but making choices has never been my strong suit.

"Call me old-fashioned," I'll say to him as I start, "but isn't it usually the guy's responsibility to ask a woman out?"

No. Weak. I'll need something punchier if I really want to go down that route. Maybe call him—

"Hey," a familiar voice says, bringing me out of my thoughts.

Oh. Great.

It's Champ, smoking a cigarette.

Grr. Since the party, I've done my best to prevent Colossus and Champ from meeting, and as a bonus, I've also been spared from having to accidentally smell Champ's horrid breath again.

Despite all the socialization training, Colossus doesn't run to Champ, but he also doesn't bark at him or anything. The puppy simply couldn't care less about this particular human, which, for this now-friendly dog, is almost equivalent to pure hate.

"I'm glad I've finally run into you," Champ says.

Finally? How often has he smoked here in the hopes of meeting us?

"Aren't you allergic?" I gesture at the dog.

Champ frowns at Colossus. "I wanted to run into *you*, not it. Not that I can inhale fur in the great outdoors."

Usually dander and saliva cause the allergies, not fur, but I don't want to needlessly prolong this conversation, so I keep quiet and look at Champ expectantly.

Champ looks furtively around before loudly whispering, "Can we talk?"

I think fast. "Sorry. Maybe another time? Colossus is thirsty, and so am I."

"Ah." Champ throws his cigarette on the ground and stomps on it with his tennis shoe. "I guess I'll catch you later."

Hopefully not. I only need to avoid him for one more day.

Heading straight for the garage, I unhook Colossus's leash and take him to the kitchen for drinks and snacks.

As we enter, I see the strategic mistake I made outside. By mentioning thirst, I all but told Champ where I was headed.

And he *really* wants to chat because here he is, pretending like he's in the kitchen by accident.

Ignoring him, I pour Colossus some water and take out a lick mat with his breakfast.

Before I can take my own food out, Champ walks over and looks around before whispering, "Can I *now* have a moment of your time?"

I breathe through my mouth. "What's up?"

"I was wondering about your... rates," Champ says, still in a whisper.

I blink at him. "My rates?" He's allergic to dogs, so why would he care?

"The price," he explains. "For... you know."

I take a step back. "I don't think I do know." And a gut feeling is telling me that I would not like to find out.

Champ advances on me, so I'm hit with his breath again and wonder how he has managed to eat so much garlic so early in the day. "I know about your trips to Bruce's bedroom... at night."

"Excuse me?" I don't think I'd be this shaken if he'd put out a cigarette on my forehead.

"Please, keep it down." He backs up a step. "I'm not saying there is anything wrong with... sex work. It's—"

My blood feels like it's about to explode. "I'm not a whore!" My hands ball into tight fists, and I'm itching to punch him right in the little bit of space between his eyes.

Champ frowns. "Why throw nasty labels around? I was just asking if you could do for me what you do for Bruce."

My nostrils flare. "I don't do sex work for him."

He rolls his eyes. "You and he are not a couple, right? He pays you, right? You sleep with him, right? Whatever you call that arrangement, I want one too, while we're still here."

I eye the knife rack and enjoy some fleeting mental images of me using the large carving one to slice into Champ's soft belly, like in a slasher movie. At my feet, I hear Colossus growling—he seems to be picking up on my murderous mood.

"Shut up," Champ snaps at Colossus and raises his foot threateningly.

That's it. Something inside me snaps, and my knee smashes into Champ's crotch.

Doubling over, Champ drops to the ground, face going green. Grabbing Colossus, I run to my room and lock the door behind me.

Purely on autopilot, I give the puppy a chew toy to play with before giving in to the fury that overwhelms me. Fury at Champ for what he said, but also at Bruce and at myself for ending up in this stupid situation:

sleeping with my boss who doesn't seem to have any intention of making this a relationship.

I don't even know what I'm doing when my hands reach for the closet door, but it seems like my body has done something I've never been able to do on my own: make a decision.

And that decision is to pack up my shit.

CHAPTER 33
BRUCE

Someone knocks on my office door just as I finish my crypto meeting.

Could it be Lilly? The warm hope in my chest makes me feel like a schoolboy with his first crush. Except if it were her, I don't think she would knock. She'd just barge in.

"Come in," I say and close my laptop.

Even though I didn't think it was Lilly, I feel a pang of disappointment when I see Mrs. Campbell.

"Hello, sir," she says, seeming pretty distraught.

I get to my feet. "What's wrong?"

She guiltily pulls out a piece of paper from her pocket. "I was about to do Lilly's laundry," she says. "And you know how I always check all pockets before sticking anything in the washer?"

Brows furrowing, I nod.

"When I saw it, I didn't mean to pry," she says. "But

your name was mentioned with some cuss words, so I—"

"How about you hand me that paper," I demand.

She takes a step forward but doesn't give up the note. "Maybe there's an explanation for this," she says. "Lilly is such a nice girl, and the two of you—"

My adrenaline spikes. "Give it to me. Now."

Eyes widening, Mrs. Campbell thrusts the paper into my hands and rushes out of the room.

I read the note, increasingly stupefied. It seems that Lilly believes me to be the worst person in the world—up there with the likes of Charles Manson, Caligula, and Pee-wee Herman.

But why? Surely, it's not based on my bedroom performance.

Then I see the reason toward the end of the letter and open my laptop to verify.

Fuck. It's true. My bank foreclosed on her parents' house.

No wonder she was so hostile toward me in the beginning. And so anti-business.

But how does that mesh with what we've been doing?

Blood leaves my face.

Is it possible she decided on the most twisted form of revenge—to get me to care for her, then read me this horrible soliloquy?

I reread the note again, anger displacing some of the shock and hurt. Then, like a masochist, I read it one more time. And once more.

After I read it for the hundredth time, I shove the paper into my pocket and stride out of the room.

Lilly and I are going to have words.

CHAPTER 34
LILLY

What the hell? A ton of my clothes are missing.

Oh. Right. I vaguely recall Prudence saying something about doing my laundry.

Fine. Whatever. It's not about the stuff. I just need my home. My space, where I can think.

Grabbing a suitcase stuffed with random crap, I head for the door—and bump into Bruce's cement-like chest.

Wow.

His eyes are like two icebergs as he looks me over. "Going somewhere?"

My hurt and anger boil over, and again, my body makes the decision for me as my tongue forms the words. "Damn right. I quit."

Immediately, I want to take it back, but it's too late. His eyes grow colder yet, and his nostrils flare.

"Oh?" His voice is razor sharp. "Tired of the charade?"

Charade? Me? Is it possible to be too emotional to understand words? Or is he accusing me of something —like welcoming Champ's gross advances?

I actually see red. "What happened was *your* fault."

Strangely, his expression warms a fraction. "It's not like I was involved, personally."

Is he trying to excuse Champ's behavior? "Speaking to you was a mistake."

Something ticks in his jaw. "Right back at you."

"Fine." I push him out of my way, feeling like I'm about to cry. "Goodbye."

CHAPTER 35
BRUCE

Colossus whines.

Fuck.

There I went and had a fight in front of him yet again.

Grabbing him, I sit on the bed that was Lilly's until a few seconds ago and stroke the heavenly fur. As the dog's eyes roll back in pleasure, I calm down as well, enough to think semi-coherent thoughts.

Like, for example, that I should be relieved she spared me the need to bring up her note, but I'm not. That I should be happy I discovered Lilly's duplicity before I felt too much, but I'm not… possibly because it's already too late.

No. No reason to waste time going down that train of thought.

I'll probably feel better if I hold on to my anger. I mean, how crazy was she acting when I walked in? It's illogical, even if I account for the fact that people's prefrontal cortex (the rational part of the brain) doesn't develop fully until twenty-five years of age, and she's only twenty-three.

Still. Now that I'm a tiny bit calmer, something about our encounter doesn't make sense.

Particularly this: why was she already leaving when I walked in? It would make a lot more sense if she'd stormed out after I gave her a piece of my mind about the note.

Something I didn't even get the chance to do.

It's almost like—

My phone rings, and my first thought is that it might be Lilly, calling to ask for her job back. And to apologize.

Fine, maybe it's more like I'm hoping it's Lilly.

The caller, however, is Mom.

I'm tempted not to pick up, but filial duty wins out.

"Mom, hi. Is everything okay?"

"Hi, Brucie," Mom says in her usual upbeat tone. In a sterner voice, she asks, "Did you get into a fight with your sister's boyfriend?"

"What?" I look at Colossus as if he might have answers.

Mom sighs. "You know Angela isn't a teen anymore, and that even back then, you were out of line when you—"

"I didn't get into a fight with her guy," I state slowly. I mean, when he asked Lilly to dance the other week, I *was* tempted, but stopping oneself is what a fully developed prefrontal cortex is for. "What gave you that idea?"

"A few minutes ago, I walked in on him getting up from the floor in the kitchen," she says. "He dodged my questions about what happened, like he was ashamed."

"That is odd."

"I know, right?" she says. "Angela also said she had no clue. Speaking of Angela, she said she's going to break up with him, and I'm glad, because you know how I've always felt about second-hand smoke and—"

I tune out the rest of what Mom says because some puzzle pieces are sliding into place, and I don't like the emerging picture one bit. Could there be a connection between the two strange events of Lilly's sudden departure and what Mom is talking about?

Setting the puppy on the floor, I tell Mom that I have to go.

"Sure, hon," she says and hangs up.

I rush to my office and pull up the surveillance footage for the kitchen.

CHAPTER 36
LILLY

I slam my front door and drop the suitcase.

As I look around, I find another reason to be pissed at Bruce: thanks to being in his mansion for so long, my place now looks like a hovel.

And I want to cry more than ever.

I'm also weirdly numb.

And still angry.

So, so angry.

How could I have been so stupid as to sleep with a guy I so recently considered my nemesis? Or to develop feelings for his dog? Just his dog, mind you. Not him. No way can it be him.

Unbidden, images of our Netflix and chill sessions appear in my mind as my chest starts to ache and pressure builds behind my eyes.

When I started to pack my stuff back at the mansion, I hoped I'd feel better when I got home, but I feel anything but. A part of me must've also hoped that Bruce would stop me—but he did nearly the opposite.

Come to think of it, that was a bit odd.

What was that bit about charades?

Also, when I told him the thing with Champ was his fault, his reply was confusing.

How did he even know what happened with Champ in the first place? I can't imagine Angela's boyfriend told on himself.

Wait. Why am I thinking about Bruce again?

He doesn't deserve it.

My phone rings, and Bruce is the first person I think of.

The caller is Prudence—and that might be for the best.

"Hi, Lilly," she says, sounding oddly guilty. "I wanted to apologize."

"For what?"

"For whatever Bruce said," she says. "After I gave him the note, I regretted doing so."

I nearly drop the phone. "What note?"

"I was about to do your laundry," Prudence says. "And I always check all the pockets before sticking anything in the washer because I once ruined Mr. Roxford's—"

"When did you give him that note?"

She tells me.

"Shit."

"Again," she says. "I'm sorry. I've worked for Mr. Roxford for—"

"It's fine. But I do have to go." With that, I hang up.

I try to recall what I wrote down, and it's not good. The idea of Bruce reading that stream of vitriol fills me with dread. Obviously, I don't mean a word of it anymore, but it's too late.

He knows about the foreclosure and thinks I hate his guts. Hence the word "charade" and the line about not being involved. He meant he doesn't personally foreclose on houses—he's got people for that.

My heart squeezes as I picture how I'd feel if our roles were reversed. No wonder he looked so pissed when he barged into my room. He must've been coming to fire me and tell me that he never wants to speak to me again, but I spared him the trouble.

Fuck.

What have I done?

How can I fix this?

Can it even *be* fixed?

I sink into the couch as the dam that was holding my tears at bay breaks.

CHAPTER 37
BRUCE

'm going to fire every single person on my useless security team. Turns out, there's no fucking way to skip through the security footage. It records on a seven-day loop, and today was day six, which means I have to fast forward through six days' worth of people chewing and drinking in the kitchen.

I choose to do it though—no matter how much I want to crawl up the walls. If I'm right in my suspicion, I owe it to Lilly.

Fucking fuck. There's fucking Champ, slurping fucking noodles.

I bang the table with my fist, which doesn't make me feel better. Then I watch through slitted eyes, and that doesn't help much either, especially when the fucker follows up the noodles with a Slurpee that he managed to get from God-knows-where.

Those things are the worst invention since asbestos and leaded gasoline. Even the name is disgusting, a concatenation of slur (like in ethnic slur) and pee—the last thing you want to think about when buying a drink.

That's another strike against my security team—the Slurpee is among many such products that are banned on my estate.

Just as I think my head is going to explode, I get to this morning's footage and slow the video down—even though I have to suffer through the horror show that is everyone's breakfast.

There. Champ walks into the kitchen for no apparent reason.

A few minutes later, Lilly and Colossus walk in.

Upping the sound, I watch and listen intently, and as I do, my fists clench painfully.

When it's over, my vision is blurred from the fury raging inside me. Using the same security system, I triangulate Champ's current location, and my legs carry me to him, almost as if they have a will of their own.

"Hey," Champ says to me when I catch up with him in the eastern hallway. "How's—"

My fist smashes into his jaw, hard. He flies up, then collapses on the ground, like the sack of shit that he is.

I wait for him to get up, planning to reenact the rest of my boxing workout.

"What the hell?" my sister demands, rushing down the hallway.

Did she see the punch?

"He's lucky I only punched him," I grit out.

"What happened?" Angela asks, forehead furrowing.

I tell her, and when I'm done, her eyes look misty, but she doesn't cry. Instead, she walks over to Champ's limp body and kicks him in the ribs. "We're fucking over!"

Champ yelps in pain.

"Get up," I order him.

Champ shakily gets to his feet. "I'm going to sue," he whines.

"Good luck," Angela says coldly. "My brother's lawyers will make burgers out of yours."

I grab Champ by his shirt collar and lift him off the ground. "You have five minutes to disappear from my estate. If you come near Lilly or my sister again, it will be the end of you."

As soon as I let go of his shirt, Champ sprints away —and I fight murderous urges as I watch him go.

"What about Lilly?" Angela asks.

"She left," I grit out, and Champ is lucky that I don't have a gun on me at this moment.

Angela frowns. "Left?"

"Quit," I say. "Me and the job."

Angela puts a reassuring hand on my shoulder. "What will you do?"

I don't even have to think about my reply. "I'm going to go get her back."

CHAPTER 38
LILLY

don't know how long I cry for; I just know that at some point, my phone rings and I force myself to stop in order to answer it.

"Hi, hon," Mom says. "I have unbelievable news."

Doing my best not to sniffle audibly, I ask, "What happened?"

"The bank called," Dad exclaims. "Oh, you're on speaker, by the way."

"The bank?" Even though that's a tenuous connection to Bruce, my chest squeezes.

"Yeah. They admitted that they made an error during our foreclosure proceedings—"

"What error?" I ask. Isn't foreclosure as simple as: when you don't pay, you lose the house?

"We didn't understand the legalese," Mom says. "But long story short, to make up for the mistake, they're giving us the house back, free and clear."

My skin breaks out in goosebumps. "Didn't the bank sell it?" And are my parents really this gullible?

"They bought it back from that family, so we can move back in a month," Dad says excitedly. "Can you believe it?"

Yeah. I believe they are getting the house. What I don't believe is the story the bank told them. What really happened is that Bruce learned about the foreclosure from my note and decided to reverse it. Which is insane. But why would he—

Someone bangs on my door, startling me.

Some sixth sense tells me who it might be—and I hope it's not wishful thinking.

"Mom, Dad, I'm very happy for you," I rattle out. "But can we talk more later? I have to run."

"To deal with her oh-so-demanding employer, no doubt," Mom says—probably to Dad.

I hang up and dash to the door to look into the peephole.

The glimmer of hope unfurls into a bright glow in my chest when I see the warm ocean-blue eyes peering back at me.

Hands shaking, I unlock the door and let Bruce in.

He seems to take up my whole place, making it seem even tinier.

"Hi," I say, heart hammering in my chest.

"Thanks for letting me in," he murmurs. "I wasn't sure—"

"I just heard from my parents," I blurt. "Did you—"

"Sorry if that was a bit heavy-handed," he says. "I

know I can't right every wrong my bank has ever done, but since I could help in this case, I figured I'd—"

"Are you apologizing for giving us back my childhood home?" I don't know if my heart palpitations are a sign of arrhythmia and therefore warrant a 9-1-1 call, or not.

"Speaking of apologies, I'm sorry about what happened with Champ." Bruce's expression darkens. "Rest assured, he will *never* bother you again. He and my sister are over, so if he—"

"They are?" I ask dumbly. "Does that mean she's going to take Colossus back?" Why did I ask that, of all things?

Bruce shakes his head. "Angela will have to get herself a new dog. Colossus is mine."

Oh, no. I feel like I'm going to start crying again, and I'm not sure why. "How did you find out about—"

"Surveillance camera in the kitchen," he says.

Ah. Right. He actually told me about it at one point.

"Is that why you've come? To tell me that?" I realize some form of this should've been my first question, but I was too afraid to ask. If he says something like, "I'm here to get you to come back to work," the geyser behind my eyes might burst forth, get him all wet, and then—

"I want you to be my girlfriend," Bruce declares solemnly. "To be with me. Be mine. Whatever terminology the kids are using these days."

I gape at him, unsure I've heard correctly.

He steps closer. "You don't have to answer now. I know a lot has happened and—"

"Yes," I say, a bit too loudly. I'm not sure if it's the heat from his body, or his scent, but I start to grow dizzy. "I'll be yours... I mean, your girlfriend. Or go steady, or whatever oldsters like you called it back in the days of yesteryear."

"Good." He steps closer, eyes gleaming. "There's something else."

I arch an eyebrow because his proximity is making my breathing too fast for coherent speech.

Bruce takes my hand and lifts it to his chest. "It's something I probably should wait to tell you. At least until we go on a few more dates and more time has passed."

"Tell me what?" I breathe.

"I love you." He gently squeezes my hand. "I love how kindhearted you are—especially with Colossus. I love your zest for life—how in such a short time, you've managed to make me appreciate what I have and even start to enjoy it. I love—"

"I do too," I blurt. "Love you, that is. And sorry to interrupt, but you just kept going on and on and—"

Our lips clash, and his kiss is as passionate as it is possessive.

The kiss tells me we're official.

It tells me I'm his.

EPILOGUE

BRUCE

I sit in a theater I've rented, surrounded by family and friends—both mine and Lilly's. Around us is a crowd of dog parents who are as proud as I am, their fluffy charges on a leash next to their chairs dressed in a custom-made graduation uniform. The dogs, that is. Although some parents are wearing a version of it too.

"Chewbacca Stevenson," Lilly says from the stage, and I hear my sister chuckle. She and Lilly often try to one up each other when it comes to inventing silly names for dogs, and *Star Wars* references are staples for both of them.

I hope that dog doesn't go by Chewie. For those with misophonia like me, that's the equivalent of calling a dog Pukie. Or Poopie. Or Noodlie.

The lady on my left beams and urges her German Shepherd (who does look like his namesake) to head over to Lilly.

When they get to her, Lilly shakes the woman's hand and asks Chewbacca to give her a paw, which he (I assume it's a he) does. Finally, Lilly hands the lady a roll of official papers, while Chewbacca gets one of the edible trophies commissioned for this specific occasion.

We all laugh as Chewbacca devours his hard-won reward.

Lilly calls the next dog, and this time, the swell of pride I feel isn't for my fur child, but for her. She's done it. She's actualized her dream, and here is the first graduating class of her new dog school—Barkshire Pawaway.

When I glance at the faces of Lilly's parents, I can see them tearing up, and I bet they share the same sentiment. And hey, they have the right to be proud. Lilly accomplished this smoothly and swiftly, mere months after officially moving in with me (not that she stayed at her own place when we were "just dating").

As Lilly calls the next graduate, she waves her toned arm, which makes me uncomfortable in the crotch area.

Not this again. I will Titan, as she calls him, to calm the fuck down by thinking of government-employed accountants eating soup.

Nope. Down is a difficult command for Titan to master when Lilly is around.

Figures. Colossus and I will get called to the stage any minute, and I'll be sporting a hard-on.

What's worse, the dogs might know that I'm

aroused. I mean, if Lilly can teach them to soothe a person when stressed, or to indicate they need an insulin shot, this seems pretty easy in comparison.

"Noodle Schwartz," Lilly says.

Wow. It's like these owners are trying to make their dogs sound horrible. At least things are cooling down for my cock—especially when I also imagine Hitler drinking a Slurpee.

"This last dog has a special place in my heart," Lilly says. "As does his owner."

Everyone around us oohs-and-aahs.

"Colossus Roxford," Lilly says. "Come here, sweeties."

As Colossus and I walk onto the stage, there's deafening clapping and cheering.

Lilly starts with the edible award first, and then as Colossus eats it, she gives me a kiss in front of everyone.

Damn it. No thoughts of noodles or even a Slurpee can tame the beastly erection that results.

When Lilly notices it, she chuckles and whispers, "Exit through the side of the stage. I'll walk with you and block *that* with my body. Or as much of it as I can, with Titan being so huge and me so tiny, of course."

We do as she says, and as soon as we're out of people's sight, I steal another kiss, even if it's counterproductive to my current situation.

Someone clears his throat.

Looking over my shoulder, Lilly chuckles again. "Johnny, can you take Colossus for a walk, please?"

Taking the leash out of my hands, she hands it to my assistant.

When we're alone, she pulls me into a dressing room and locks the door.

All right. I strip off our clothes and make frantic love to her—with my hand muffling her passionate screams in case anyone is on the other side of the paper-thin walls.

Afterward, Lilly fixes her hair and picks up her bra. "Who knew the graduation ceremony would be such a potent aphrodisiac?"

"Your mere presence does it for me," I say. "And congrats, again."

I grab my phone and let my assistant know he can come back with Colossus—and that he should bring codename "Big Surprise" with him at the same time.

By the time we're dressed, there's a knock on the door.

"I got you something," I tell Lilly. "Something, or rather *someone*, that I think you will like."

Lilly's eyebrows—which I've secretly named Borat and Super Mario—become animated, like they're just begging for me to kiss them again.

But I won't, as that could lead to another sex session, and we have company.

Speaking of… "Come in," I say.

They do, and Lilly gapes at codename "Big Surprise." On a gasp, she asks, "Is that another Chihuahua?"

"Correct." I grin. "I got her from a shelter earlier

today. While you thought Colossus and I were having that long walk. And in case you're worried, the two of them loved each other at first sight."

I gesture a dismissal at my assistant, and as he leaves, Lilly envelops the tiny puppy in a hug. "Did you name her?"

I shake my head. "Figured you'd like to do the honors."

She scratches the puppy under her furry chin. "What do you think of Gargantua?"

I look the puppy over again. She has the light-brown smooth coat made famous by Paris Hilton's companion and Taco Bell commercials. "That name seems derivative of Colossus, but more importantly, Gargantua was the name of a *male* giant."

Lilly sticks her tongue out at me. "Spencer is a boy's name, but if I have a baby girl, that's what I'll call her."

She's playing with fire there because if given the chance, I'd put a baby girl—or boy—in her in a heartbeat, but she's not there just yet.

"How about you brainstorm names with Angela later today?" I suggest.

After a rocky start, and to my surprise, these two very different women have become good friends.

Lilly grins. "She'd love that, but I think I have a name. Roach."

"Ah," I say. "Perfect."

"There's actually something else," I say. "Pertaining to my sister."

Lilly turns Borat into a facsimile of a question mark.

"I've finally decided what my hobby will be," I say. "And Angela will help me with it."

"Ah. You've finally realized that giving me orgasms isn't a *real* hobby." Lilly winks at me. "Not that I don't appreciate it."

I pull her close but resist kissing her lips for the moment since that would be detrimental to speaking.

"I'm opening a dog rescue," I say, looking into her eyes. "On the estate."

Borat and Super Mario shoot up Lilly's forehead excitedly. "I love that!" she exclaims. "I really, really do."

"And I love you," I say and claim her lips in the most passionate kiss of all.

SNEAK PEEKS

Thank you for participating in Lilly and Bruce's journey!

Can't get enough of animal-loving billionaires?
Check out *Billionaire Rake*, a fake marriage romance featuring a book-obsessed heroine and the hot single dad who sweeps her off her feet (or should we say, his dog does…literally).

Need more enemies-to-lovers? Read *The Love Deal*! When Honey gets caught making fraudulent coupons, she has two options: jail time or a job that requires her to work for her high school nemesis. Is there really a difference?

Try our other laugh-out-loud romcoms:

- *Hard Code*

- *Hard Ware*
- *Hard Byte*
- *Royally Tricked*
- *Femme Fatale-ish*
- *Of Octopuses and Men*
- *Sextuplet and the City*
- *Billionaire Grump*

We love receiving feedback from our readers, and we are always interested to know what you'd like to see in books to come. Want your favorite side character to have their own book? Mention it in a review! We take all suggestions into consideration, and if you sign up for our newsletter at www.mishabell.com, you'll be the first to know who will be featured next!

Misha Bell is a collaboration between husband-and-wife writing team, Dima Zales and Anna Zaires. When they're not making you bust a gut as Misha, Dima writes sci-fi and fantasy, and Anna writes dark and contemporary romance. Check out *Wall Street Titan* by Anna Zaires for more steamy billionaire hotness!

Turn the page to read previews from *Billionaire Grump* and *The Love Deal*!

EXCERPT FROM BILLIONAIRE GRUMP

BY MISHA BELL

Juno

When I'm late for a job interview and get stuck on an elevator with an annoyingly sexy, Ancient Rome-obsessed grump, the last thing I expect is for him to be the billionaire owner of the building. I also don't expect to almost kill him… accidentally, of course.

Sure, I don't get the plant care position I applied for, but I do receive an interesting offer.

Lucius needs to trick the public (and his grandma) into thinking he's in a relationship, and I need tuition money to get my botany degree. Our arrangement is mutually beneficial—that is, until I start catching feelings.

If being a cactus lover has taught me anything, it's that

if you get too close, there's a good chance you'll end up hurt.

Lucius

Post-elevator incident, I'm left with three things: my favorite water bottle full of pee, a life threatening allergic reaction, and paparazzi photos of my "girl-friend" and I that make my Gram the happiest woman alive.

Naturally, my next step is to blackmail—I mean, convince—this (admittedly cute) girl to pretend to date me. That way, my grandma stays happy, and as a bonus, I can keep the gold diggers at bay.

Unfortunately, my arch nemesis, a.k.a. biology, kicks in, and the whole "not getting physical" part of our agreement becomes increasingly hard to abide by. Worse yet, the longer I'm with Juno, the more my delicately crafted icy exterior melts away.

If I'm not careful, Juno will tear down my walls completely.

———

"Are you calling me stupid?" I snap. Anyone could have trouble with these damn buttons, not just a person with dyslexia.

He looks pointedly at the buttons. "Stupid is as stupid does."

I grind my teeth, painfully. "You're an asshole. And you've watched *Forrest Gump* one too many times."

His lips flatten. "That movie wasn't the origin of that saying. It's from Latin: *Stultus est sicut stultus facit.*"

I roll my eyes. "What kind of pretentious *stultus* quotes Latin?"

The steel in his eyes is so cold I bet my tongue would get stuck if I tried to lick his eyeball. "I don't know. Maybe the 'idiot' who happens to like everything related to Rome, including their numerals."

My jaw drops open. "You made this decision?" I wave toward the elevator buttons.

He nods.

Shit. He probably heard me earlier, which means I started the insults. In my defense, he did make an idiotic choice.

I exhale a frustrated breath. "If you're such an expert on Roman numerals, you could've told me which one to press."

He crosses his arms over his chest. "You didn't ask me."

My hackles rise again. "Ask you? You looked like you might bite my head off for just existing."

"That's because you delayed—"

The elevator jerks to a stop, and the lights around us dim.

We both stare at the doors.

They stay shut.

He turns to me and narrows his eyes accusingly. "What did you press now?"

"Me? How? I've been facing you. Unfortunately."

With an annoying headshake, he stalks toward the panel with the buttons, and I have to leap away before I get trampled.

"You probably pressed something earlier," he mutters. "Why else would we be stuck?"

Why is it illegal to choke people? Just a few seconds with my hands on his throat would be a calming exercise.

Instead, I glare at his back, which is blocking my view of what he's doing, if anything. "The poor elevator probably just committed suicide over these Roman numerals. It knew that when someone sees things like L and XL, they think of T-shirt sizes for Neanderthal types like you. And don't get me started on that XXX button, which is a clear reference to porn. It creates a hostile work env—"

"Can you shut up so I can get us out of this?" he snaps.

His words bring home the reality of our situation: it's been over a minute, and the doors are still closed.

Dear saguaro, am I really stuck here? With this guy? What about my interview?

"Silence, finally," he says with satisfaction and moves to the side, so I see him jam his finger at the "help" button.

"It's a miracle that's not in Latin," I can't help but say. "Or Klingon."

"Hello?" he says into the speaker under the button, his voice dripping with irritation.

No reply, not even static.

"Anyone there?" His annoyance is clearly rising to new heights. "I'm late for an important meeting."

"And I'm late for an interview," I chime in, in case it matters.

He pauses to arch a thick eyebrow at me. "An interview? For what position?"

I stand straighter. "I'm sure the likes of you don't realize this, but the plants in this building don't take care of themselves."

Wait. Have I said too much? Could he torpedo my interview—assuming this elevator snafu hasn't done it already? What does he do here, anyway—design ridiculous elevators? That can't be a full-time job, can it?

"A tree hugger," he mutters under his breath. "That tracks."

What an asshole. I've never hugged a tree in my life. I'm too busy talking to them.

He returns his scowling attention to the "help" button—though now I'm thinking it should've been labeled as "no help."

"Hello? Can you hear me?" he shouts. "Answer now, or you're fired."

I roll my eyes. "Is it a good idea to be a dick to the person who can save us?"

He blows out an audible breath. "It doesn't matter. The button must be malfunctioning. They wouldn't dare ignore me."

I pull out my trusty phone, a nice and simple Nokia 3310. "Full of yourself much?"

He stares at my hands incredulously. "So that's why the elevator got stuck. It went through a time warp and transported us to 2008."

I frown at the lack of reception on my Nokia. "This version was released in 2017."

"It still looks dumber than a brain-dead crash test dummy." He proudly pulls an iPhone from his pocket. "*This* is what a phone should look like."

I scoff. "That's what constant distraction looks like. Anyway, if your iNotSoSmartPhone—trademarked—is so great, it should have some reception, right?"

He glances at his screen, but I can tell he already knows the truth: no reception for his darling either.

Still, I can't resist. "See? Your genius of a phone is just as useless. All it's good for is turning people into social-media-checking zombies."

He hides the device, like a protective parent. "On top of all your endearing qualities, you're a techno-phobe too?"

I debate throwing my Nokia at his head but decide it's not worth shelling out sixty-five bucks for a replacement. "Just because I don't want to be distracted doesn't mean I'm a technophobe."

"Actually, my phone is great at blocking out distrac-tions." He puts the headphones back over his ears. "See?" He presses play, and I hear the faint riffs of heavy metal.

"Very mature," I mouth at him.

"Sorry," he says overly loudly. "I can't hear any distractions."

Fine. Whatever. At least he has good taste in music. My cactus and I are big fans of Metallica, which is what I think he's listening to.

I begin to pace back and forth.

I'm stuck, and I'm late. If this elevator jam doesn't resolve itself in the next minute or two, I can pretty much kiss the new job goodbye—and by extension, my tuition money. No tuition money means no botany degree, which has been my dream for the last few years.

By saguaro's juices, this sucks really bad.

I sneak a glance at the hottie—I mean, asshole.

What would he say about someone with dyslexia wanting a college degree? Probably that I'd need a university that uses coloring books. In truth, even coloring books wouldn't help that much—I can never stay inside those stupid lines.

I sigh and look away, increasingly worried. My dreams aside, what if the elevator stays stuck for a while?

The most immediate problem is my growing need to pee—but paradoxically, a longer-term worry will be finding liquids to drink.

I wonder... If you're thirsty enough, does your body reabsorb the water from the bladder? Also, could I MacGyver a filter to reclaim the water in my urine with what I have on me? Maybe through cat hair?

I shiver, and only partially from the insane AC

that's somehow reaching me even in here. In the short term, it would be so much better if it were hot instead of cold. I'd sweat out the liquids and not need to pee, though I guess I'd die of thirst sooner. I sneak an envious glance at the large stranger. I bet he has a bladder the size of a blimp. He also has a stainless-steel bottle that's probably filled with water that he likely won't share.

There's also the question of food. I don't have anything edible with me, apart from a can of cat food… and, theoretically, the cat herself.

No. I'd sooner eat this stranger than poor Atonic.

As if psychic, the stranger's stomach growls.

Crap. With this guy being so big and mean, he'd probably eat the cat. After that, he'd eat me… and not in a fun way.

I'm so, so screwed.

———

Visit www.mishabell.com to order your copy of *Billionaire Grump* today!

EXCERPT FROM THE LOVE DEAL

BY MISHA BELL

Honey Hyman (do NOT call her "hon") is all leather, piercings, and tattoos. And yes, she may be just a tad deal-obsessed, but who isn't? It's not like her using coupons is stealing from anyone... unless, of course, those coupons are the fakes she created to help her elderly neighbors afford groceries from the Munch & Crunch, the uber-expensive supermarket that's replaced their local grocery store.

It really isn't fair for her to go to jail. Or to be black-mailed into working for the Munch & Crunch CEO whom she's supposedly defrauded—a CEO who turns out to be none other than Gunther Ferguson, her high school crush who once ruined both her school record and her life.

Let the war begin.

———

The police? What the hell?

Heart thumping, I check the peephole.

Yep. They're dressed like cops.

Did a neighbor call them because of the caterwauling? It did sound like bloody murder. But how did they get here so fast? Unless…

Fuck. It can't be about the coupons again, can it?

"Open the door, or we'll be forced to open it," a hard-faced cop says.

Well, shit. I can't afford to repair this door.

There's no choice.

I open the door.

The cop looks from me to Pearl. "Honey Hyman?"

"That's me." And yes, I know my name sounds like a virginal membrane that people with diabetes should avoid.

"You're under arrest," he informs me. "For fraud."

My stomach drops. I turn to Pearl, who is as pale as the ghost of a toilet. My voice is strained as I say, "Let Blue know, okay?"

Blue is our clutch mate who used to work for the government, so if anyone can help with this, it would be her.

The rest is like a nightmare. I'm led out of the building, put in a police car, brought unceremoniously into the station, and shepherded into a room—all the while fielding a surge of adrenaline so strong I barely register any of it.

Did someone read me my Miranda Rights? If not, do I get a refund?

They didn't take my butterfly knife, which is weird because I always thought going to jail was like flying on a plane—weapons aren't allowed.

Maybe I'm not going to jail? Dare I hope?

I think back on the last two times I was in trouble. Both were actually interrelated situations.

First, there was Tiffany, a cheerleader who bullied me for ogling her uber-hot boyfriend, Gunther—something I *was* guilty of. Eventually, I stood up to her with a knife—only as a threat, though, since the last thing I wanted was to draw any blood. Unfortunately, the dumdum didn't notice said knife and got up in my face anyway, accidentally slicing her arm open. To this day, I don't know how bad the cut was, as I couldn't look at the wound on account of the blood. Since Tiffany didn't end up with a scar, I imagine the cut wasn't so bad—not that it helped me escape the resulting suspension and mark on my permanent record. On the bright side, that incident is what started my "don't mess with me" reputation, which I don't mind at all, as it has kept the other Tiffanies of the world away.

The second incident took place a year later, still in high school. It involved Gunther again—who was no longer with Tiffany at the time. Not that I kept track. Much. That time, not only did I get suspended and *really* tarnish my permanent record, but I also barely dodged the juvenile justice system.

It all started when I was little. For whatever reason,

I became obsessed with all things saving money, including deals and coupons. After taking an art class my junior year, I realized that tweaking percentages on coupons with a white pen was just as profitable as counterfeiting money—so I did it, first for myself and then for the other kids at my school. As it turned out, one of the stores that lost money because of my creative initiative was owned by Gunther's family, so when Gunther learned of my activities, he tattled to the principal. Shit hit the fan, and I'm paying for it to this day.

My phone rings.

Huh. Another thing they didn't take.

I check it.

It's Blue. Good. Pearl must've told her to get in touch.

"Hi," I say, switching to a form of Pig Latin Blue developed when we were kids. "Let's talk quick. They might come back and take my phone."

"The quick version is, whatever they have against you is physical, not digital, so there's not much I can do here," Blue says.

Blue hasn't had any trouble with the law, but she doesn't seem to have much respect for certain legalities after working for—as she calls it—"No Such Agency." Case in point: she's just admitted to hacking into the police department's computers as casually as I'd admit to watching cat videos on TikTok.

"Can your former colleagues help?" I ask.

"Sorry, no," she says. "I know some feds, but that

doesn't help your case. If you want, I can text you the name of an excellent lawyer."

"Sure." Except I have no idea how I'd pay said lawyer. Thanks to my high school mishaps, no college wanted me, and I never achieved my dream of becoming a wealthy business owner. Currently, I work part-time sweeping floors at a tattoo parlor and cutting hair at a barbershop.

"I can lend you some money," Blue says, clearly reading my mind.

"No." I hate charity. "I'll take the public attorney."

"It's coupons again, isn't it?" she whispers.

"I'm not sure I should talk about it," I whisper back. "Even in code."

I hear her type a few keystrokes. Then she whispers, "You don't need to say anything. I just checked, and the answer is yes."

Fuck. I want to smack myself. After years of walking the straight and narrow, I got tempted to play Robin Hood, and this is the result. My neighborhood family-owned grocery store was recently replaced by the uber-expensive Munch & Crunch supermarket, and my elderly neighbors told me that they're struggling to afford food. So I fudged a few coupons for them. Why is that even a crime?

"Someone is coming your way," Blue says, startling me out of my reverie. "Talk later."

Before I can wonder how she knows that, she hangs up and the door opens.

I gape at the man who walks in. The epitome of tall,

dark, and handsome, he has neatly cut, smoothed-back brown hair that makes me think of corporate board-rooms and OCD. His strong chin and muscular jaw are clean-shaven to the point of shine, and his eyes, a vivid emerald-green two shades brighter than mine, are narrowed with disapproval, his full lips pursed tight.

Who is he, and why does he look familiar?

In that perfectly tailored suit, he's unlikely to be a cop. Perhaps a lawyer that I can't afford? It's possible, but there's something annoyingly honest and noble in his features that I associate more with Boy Scouts than with ambulance chasers.

"Honey Hyman," he says with distaste—and shock rolls through me as I recognize his deliciously deep baritone, one he's had since his teenage years.

"Gunther Ferguson?" I blurt incredulously.

Is it possible that I conjured him up by thinking of him on the way here, kind of like invoking a demon? Or maybe I fell asleep in the police car and I'm dreaming?

If not, then this man is what happened to the boy I hate, the one who got me into trouble in high school, thus proving that karma is a fucking myth. If there were any justice in the world, he would've grown warped and deformed with time, like an evil lord of the Sith, but the opposite has happened.

Like an Anne Rice vampire, the evil transformation has made him hotter.

"Is playing dumb your latest game?" Gunther pulls out a stack of coupons and tosses them on the table.

"Are you going to pretend you didn't know that it's my store you've been stealing from?"

Stunned, I glance down.

Yep. Those expertly faked coupons are for that small-business-crushing Munch & Crunch. And indeed, they are my handywork—but that store is part of a multinational chain of supermarkets, so how can it be his? Unless...

"You own that Munch & Crunch, like a franchise?" I ask stupidly.

He scoffs. "I own the whole company. Like you didn't know that."

I blink. "How would I know that?"

He gestures at the coupons. "The same way you know how to make those look indistinguishable from the real thing."

Hold on. Is he just a clever cop? "I'm not about to incriminate myself. Assuming those are actually fake, I'm sure whoever created them did it to help out their elderly neighbors who used to shop at the place that your Munch & Crunch ruthlessly drove out of business. Those folks can't afford your regular prices. In any case, how could that mystery person know that you had anything to do with the store? I know the likes of you think you're the center of the universe, but that's just not true."

He sighs. "First, you did this same thing to my dad. Now me. If this isn't targeted, I have to assume you make so many fraudulent coupons that this has inexorably happened again."

I push the coupons away. "Not admitting anything —but what about bad luck?"

His full lips curl in a sneer. "I don't believe in luck."

"Oh, luck exists." Bad luck is the only thing that can explain how tempting his mouth looks—despite what it's saying.

"You can prevaricate as much as you want, but the case against you is airtight. In fact, I've been led to believe you'll face jail this time. Unless…"

Wait. Is this blackmail? "Unless what?"

A dozen naughty scenarios of what he might demand of me play out in my mind—some involving handcuffs (because police station), others candle wax (no idea why), and a bunch more featuring a bed covered in BOGO coupons.

His green eyes gleam triumphantly. "Unless you work for me. Then I'll drop the charges."

———

Visit www.mishabell.com to order your copy of *The Love Deal* today!

ABOUT THE AUTHOR

We love writing humor (often the inappropriate kind), happy endings (both kinds), and characters quirky enough to be called oddballs (because... balls). If you love your romance heavy on the comedy and feel-good vibes, visit www.mishabell.com and sign up for our newsletter.

Made in the USA
Middletown, DE
20 November 2023